HIGH PRIESTESS OF ATLANTIS

Book Two Of The Priestess Chronicles

JULIEN DUBROW

Published By Julien DuBrow Ventures
San Francisco, California

Published by Julien DuBrow Ventures: www.JulienDuBrow.com

Book Cover Images by Helena Nelson-Reed: www.fine-art-studios.com

Map by Brenden Hickey: rednecter@hotmail.com

ISBN: 978-1-7352164-1-6

First Printing, 2018
Second Printing, 2020

For my mother, Diana, my best friend.

"She is the fragrance of Rose,
all she touches is made holy.
Her anointing abides as blessing within me,
all the days of my life.

Logos Sophia

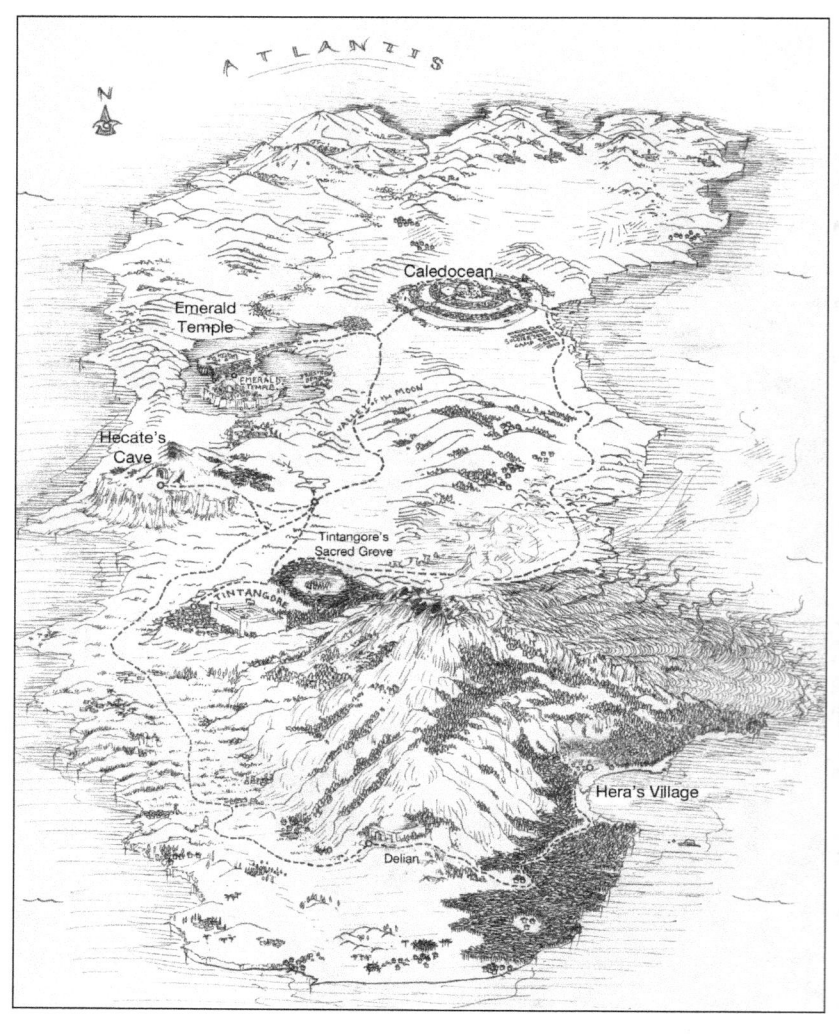

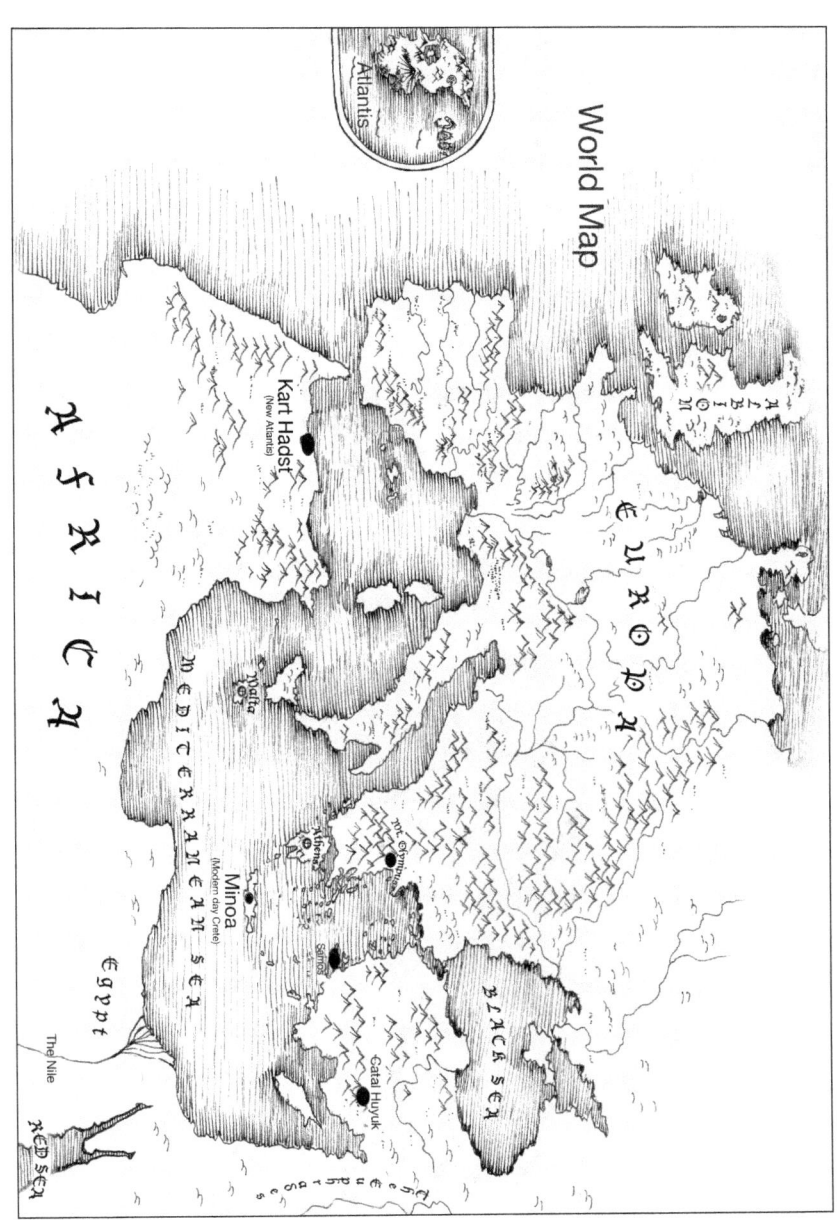

World Map

Atlantis

AFRICA

EUROPA

MEDITERRANEAN SEA

Kart Hadsr
(New Atlantis)

Natfa

Minoa
(Modern day Crete)

Minoa

Mt. Olympus

Samos

Çatal Huyuk

BLACK SEA

Egypt

The Nile

RED SEA

HERA SPEAKS

I AM OLD NOW, ANCIENT, but the heart of a priestess still beats within my chest. The memories come back to me now, strong and clear as I look into the fire, and call them forth.

I have told you how I was raised in the small village on the Eastern shore of Atlantis, and how it had been hidden from me that my mother was a priestess, heir to the High Priestess of the Emerald Temple. I have told you how the affinity with the element of fire, long buried in my lineage, had been awakened within me, and how this set in motion the events that took me to the Emerald Temple for training in the arts of the priestess. In the telling, you have come to know me as a young woman ruled by her desires, often reckless, and defiant and afraid. When my time at the Emerald Temple came to an end, when, in a moment of rage I lost control of the fire element, scorching my sister priestess, my youth ended.

I was sent away from the Emerald Temple and taken to the initiatory time of my life. It was that moment that comes to us all when we will choose our path and greet with courage whatever we meet as we walk it.

On the day I rode away from the Emerald Temple, I knew that I rode forward toward a significant change within myself. I cannot say I was not afraid, or that sadness over leaving my sister priestesses did not arise, but I knew that what I was moving towards would make me into the woman I still longed to be.

And so, I mounted Pegasus, my beloved stallion, and followed Athena through the mist, away from the temple. We crossed Atlantis' fertile plains. She led me far away from the great city of Caledocean, and the dynastic clans, and priests, who would, one day, stand against me, and the feminine face of the divine that I would serve.

We traveled undercover, and by night when the moon would lend us her light. When we reached the Western shore, we skirted the remote villages, until we came upon an ancient grove that grew just beside the sea. I felt the power of the place long before we reached it. Thick Banyan trees spread out their ancient limbs, entwining with one another like old lovers. A thin trail, overgrown with shrubs and blackberry vines, wound its way up the hill behind the grove. Spring flowers grew in rich patches of blossom all along the incline that led to the cave of Hecate, priestess of the cycles of life and death... my *Teacher*.

CHAPTER ONE

A BIRD WAS SINGING somewhere outside the cave, and the morning light fell in dim rays on the open hearth. Hecate sat on the log at its side, pushing the embers back and forth with a big stick. The fire crackled and spat as it stirred into flame.

I arched my body, stretching my limbs, which were stiff from the cold and damp of my first night in the cave. I had arrived alone, in the dark, having left my guide, Athena, in the sacred grove below. I was tired from the many days of travel, and the journey on foot up the steep, narrow trail that led to the cave. I had led Pegasus up the roughly trodden path, scored by the tracks of sheep and goats. When we reached the top Hecate was waiting for me, an oil lamp in hand. She greeted me warmly and led me to the small paddock, which would be Pegasus' home and then took me to her cave. She gave me warm stew to eat then let me lay down by the fire. That was the last thing I remembered.

Now, I looked around the small cave. I was lying on a bed of straw wrapped in my woolen shawl and covered with sheepskins roughly sewn together. There were lengthy rugs laid out on the ground around the hearth and an old table and chairs, covered with scrolls. Wax candles hung on drying racks set against the far wall and several chests and barrels too. Large wooden bowls of flowers and herbs were spread out on a long, stone plinth. Everywhere was a sweet, earthy smell, which made me think of mountain trails, and spring, and young lovers. I smiled at the simplicity of this place. It was vastly different from the grandeur and comfort of the Emerald Temple in which I'd spent most of the last year.

"You're awake," Hecate said. "Good, we can begin your training."

I turned my head to see her smiling, warmly.

Hecate leaned heavily on her walking stick and stood. She was an elder, maybe fifty or sixty years or even more, I couldn't tell. Her features seemed to change with the light. Her skin was very dark and taunt, like a young woman. The lines that stretched out from beside her eyes and down her cheeks looked like thin webs spun from laughter. She was clad in a simple, coarse brown cloth; her cloak, made of sheepskin and wool was pulled close about her. The boots she wore showed rents in several places.

As she moved closer to me, I caught the scent of freshly pressed lavender, which rose from the thin sprig of it, which lay behind her ear.

Hecate knelt down beside me; her hair fell in long, knotted strands that she pulled away from her face with an ivory stick and a knot on the back of her head. Reaching out, she placed her warm, rough palm on my forehead. With the other hand, she reached out and touched my wrist. To my surprise, my asp, Medusa, who'd been coiled warm against my skin, slithered down my arm and into her hand. The snake pressed herself beneath Hecate's sleeve and disappeared.

"Old friend," Hecate cooed as Medusa coiled up her arm

and laid herself on Hecate's shoulders.

I lifted my brows for Medusa had not left my body since she had chosen me in the sanctuary of the Emerald Temple.

Hecate seemed not to notice.

"Now, Hera, shut your eyes and rest and return to your dreaming. Tell me, what did you dream of last night?"

I did as she asked, laying back down, trying to grasp at images—horses charging neck to neck, men with swords, a woman on a hill, her axe above her head—but they were random and had no meaning to me. I yawned, opening my eyes as the pale light of dawn stretched itself across the sky outside the vast opening of the cave. The last images left me.

Hecate wasn't satisfied. She got back to her feet and prodded me with her walking stick, mumbling my mother's name.

"Sophia, Sophia," she muttered, shaking her head, "you did not teach the girl the most important skill," she went on as she moved back toward the fire.

Pushing away the sheepskin I stood up as well, shivering. I pulled on my leggings and found my bag to retrieve a thicker cloak. Then Hecate signaled me to take a seat beside her by the fire.

"How can it be that your mother did not teach you to dream?" she said.

"I dream, Lady Hecate," I said trying to keep a tone of deference in my voice.

She spat in the fire making it hiss.

"This is not dreaming," she said, waving her hand toward my bed of straw. "You can't remember anything worth telling, nor did you have control of dream state. This will not do. You must learn how to dream."

I reached my hands out toward the fire as she lifted the pot of water to the hot stone in the middle, setting it to boil.

"Your mother," she continued. "She was a great dreamer, maybe the finest of your line," she said. Her voice was sharp, but her face had a soft, winsome look that showed great kindness and something else.

"You knew my mother," I ventured.

She smiled. "Oh yes, that one," she said. "What a love. What a very great love, indeed."

I was taken aback by her words. I had never heard a priestess speak so frankly and with such affection. She turned to me and patted my knee.

"It does no one any good to close their heart," she said, pointing to my chest. "That is the place all true power arises from."

I smiled and nodded. "Yes Lady," I said.

"Do not call me that," she said. "I am only Hecate."

She leaned over the pot with a big ladle and poured hot water into two mugs. From somewhere beneath her cloak she pulled a handful of herbs and let them fall in each cup. She handed one to me. Steam rose from the water, and the scents warmed me as I breathed them in.

"You must follow in your mother's footsteps. You *must* learn how to dream, Hera! That is the first lesson," she said as she sipped her brew.

"But Lady," I started then dropped my eyes and began again. "I mean, Hecate, I do dream, even the waking dream. *You* know this is true!" I would never have said such a thing to a teacher before, but the ease and intimacy of the moment and Hecate's welcoming made it so easy to do. I was speaking of the night of my first journey into the waking dream when I'd first encountered Hecate in her dream form as well. She had been there and led me through the dream-like state that took me, for the first time, to the Emerald Temple.

Hecate looked at me sideways, and a long, thin smirk crept across her lips. Then she was laughing, and slapping my knee.

"You are right, my dear, of course, you are!" and she laughed, and laughed until I was laughing too.

We quieted and sat together sipping the tea for a long moment. I wiped the sleep out of the corners of my eyes, and Hecate stared at me mildly.

"You know, that is not dreaming," she said.

"But I was asleep," I replied. "I shut my eyes and lifted out of my body and came to you!"

She shook her head. "You were given an herb to drink," she said. "It helped you lift out of yourself, but dreaming, real dreaming Hera, is done at will, and the dreamer is in control, not the dream!"

I nodded my head and finished my tea.

"There is much for you to learn, but dreaming is the first and most important thing. Once you can control the dream, you will be free."

I did not understand, but I said nothing, determined to be a good student. I had to learn the kind of control that the priestesses had, and though I could not imagine how dreaming would accomplish this, I would try.

As if she had read my mind, Hecate leaned on her stick and stood.

"You are eternal," she said. "You are the spirit, the consciousness that runs the body. You are the formless intelligence that runs the form. Once you perceive that in the dream..." She drew in a long breath and shrugged. Waving her hand lightly over the fire the flames crackled and then they were gone. I stared in astonishment at the flameless hearth.

I opened my mouth to speak but thought better of it. I was now quite confident Hecate could read my mind, too.

Every morning it was the same. Hecate woke me before dawn and commanded me to retell my dream. It wasn't long before the images held fast in my mind, and the scenes replayed themselves beneath my closed eyes. The old dream of the dark-haired man and the sea came to me again on the thirteenth night, and I told it to Hecate in detail, describing the mist and the intense hue of his eyes.

"And the feeling you have toward him?" she asked.

I felt flustered and searched for words to answer her honestly, but the thought of sharing such a strong sensual pull with my teacher—

"Come, girl, hold nothing back. The dream, the dream!"

"I'm...drawn to him," I began, wanting to appease her. "He's familiar to me."

"Familiar, how?"

"I can't say it is just a feeling. It's as though I've met him, or looked into those eyes before. But I don't think I have..."

"No, no Hera, trust the feeling, don't try and figure it out. If you dream with him again, I want you to try and move toward him, to reach out with your hands and touch him."

This was a fascinating idea, and I smiled at the thought.

"But how do I do it?" I asked.

She reached out and took my hands in hers and began to rub them gently between her palms.

"It's all about awareness, Hera. You must wake up inside your dream. Set your mind to the task and it will not fail you." She rubbed my hands harder so that they grew very warm. Pleasing sensations moved up my arms and skin. "Waking up in the dream requires you to perceive that you are dreaming. It's just a matter of shifting your awareness. Right now, you're aware that I'm speaking to you. You're concentrating on what I'm saying, but at the same time, you're conscious of my touch as well. The same way you can move your focus from the sound of my voice to the sensation of my touch is the way you move from being an unconscious observer to a participant in your dream."

Hecate's instructions were simple. She sent me about the chores of the day but bade me pay attention to sensations, feelings, thoughts and impulses and the vast array of sound that filled our little plateau. I'd be stirring the stew, and she'd say, "Hera, what do you hear?" and suddenly my attention would expand to the sounds of the grouse in a nearby thicket or the cry of a hawk ready to dive down toward her prey. I was confused that Hecate gave me no meditations or chants or rituals. Instead, she had me work.

I built a new damn in the stream and widened our swimming hole. I collected wood and brush and dragged them to our shed to keep them dry for the winter. I mended clothes, fed animals, tended the garden and helped make herbal tinctures and all the while Hecate was my friendly guide.

It went on like this for days and weeks and months. I grew used to the routine and Hecate's daily questions, "Hera, what do you smell? What do you taste? How do you feel? Who are you?"

Then one night I dreamed of the blue-eyed man again.

He was standing alone on the prow of a ship, the sun very bright on his face. I seemed to be hovering above him, as if I was a cloud, watching when suddenly he turned his gaze upward, and I caught the clarity of his eyes. A shock moved through me, and I was immediately aware that I was dreaming. The sensation of being a watcher faded as I focused on his eyes. My will began to manipulate the scene. I moved down towards him, and he stepped back, gripping the rail as if he could see me too. My feelings grew intense and excited. I wanted to reach out, to touch him, to speak, and see his face more clearly, but as the force of my desire to interact grew, the dream began to fade, and I opened my eyes in the darkness of the cave. A terrible sense of regret and loneliness swept over me.

That morning, when I told Hecate what happened, I could hear the sadness and longing in my voice.

"Give it time, Hera," she counseled. "It takes a priestess many years to hone the dreaming skill. You're already very gifted. In time, it will come."

I nodded and got to my feet. I pulled my cloak from the trunk at the foot of my sleeping place and stepped outside to build a fire in the big, outdoor hearth. This is where we did most of our cooking and the brewing of herbs. Hecate followed as I piled on the wood, and dried leaves, and reached for the flint.

"Wait," Hecate said, stepping very close, kneeling beside me. She took my wrist and held my hand over the fire pit. "You're aware of your feelings right now, of your disappointment, but there is something else happening inside you, Hera ..." She let go of my hand and sat back. My palm faced the kindling. "Hera, you're too focused on your emotions. *Notice them but don't let your mind indulge in them.* Other things are happening within you as well. What else are you aware of?"

I pursed my lips and concentrated on my body.

My hand was hot. A strong pulling sensation tugged at my chest and seemed to spiral down my arm.

"Let the fire come," Hecate whispered. "Rest your awareness on what *is* within you right now, not on what you wish it to be."

I felt a sharp spiked sensation, and my fingers trembled as I let go of the dream of the blue-eyed man and my desire for connection and success.

"You are the formless consciousness that runs the form. From that place, reach out to the fire in its formless state and call it into form."

My hand shook as an orange spark leapt from the wood beneath my palm, and turned into flame. I pulled my hand away and fell backward abruptly.

Hecate rose to her feet. "There is no greater quest than the one to find your True Self, Hera," she said. "Now, make us something warm to eat."

Time passed slowly. The dream came now and then, but I could never manipulate it. On some nights I found my way into the landscape of my dreams and learned to maintain my sense of self amid the changing scenes. As this ability deepened, my control over my emotions and the fire gift grew. And all the while, Hecate taught me to harness and hone my intuitive skills beneath her watchful eye. She wasn't sharp, or contrite, as Athena had been, but she didn't offer a conversational companionship either. Though I found my studies engaging and would not turn away from the mysteries unfolding before me, I was also aware of an increasing sense of loneliness and melancholy that would not leave me.

Throughout the Spring I stayed with Hecate, occupied by our daily work and lessons, but as time went on, I missed the companionship of my peers. I missed the conversations, the merriment, and the romantic confidences and hopes. I often felt very alone.

When I shared this with Hecate, she looked startled.

"You feel alone?" she said. "What do you mean, Hera?"

We were standing on the high green plateau studded with solitary trees that were stark, and misshapen by the steady salt air and wind. There were shrubs all about us bursting with white flowers. The hummingbirds and bees flitted from one the next, and somewhere high above us, the light, dazzling song of a lark floated on the wind.

Hecate glanced about us as if for the first time. She stretched out her arms as if receiving someone.

"I have been too long with all my senses open," she said. "Forgive me, I forget." Her eyes lifted to the sky as it filled with light and she exhaled, laughing. "I hear the song that the sun sings when it rises, and it has become the voice of an old friend. The rocks speak to me, and the trees," she pointed toward the gnarled-trunked figures that surrounded the green, "They've been my companions for such a long time, and such stories they tell."

She reached out her hand and Medusa, who'd taken to lying gracefully about Hecate's neck, moved down her arm and toward me. I reached out absently to take my serpent. I was comforted by the slight weight of her body as she took her place about my shoulders.

"Well, we must fix this. I have need of supplies for the coming season. Winter will be here soon. You can take the pony into the village each new moon and trade for what we need. Just tell the women in the market that you are my niece come to look after me. They'll put you up and take care of you while you stay."

Forgetting all decorum I put my arms around Hecate's neck. She let out another emphatic laugh and let me kiss her cheeks before I pulled away.

"Youth," she said, the lines around her eyes creasing in delight. "I'd forgotten what youth is like as well! What an enchantment."

I shook my head, "You're not *that* old!" I said letting her go.

"Perhaps," she replied, the smile fading from her lips. "But I'm older then you think, Hera."

I took up her hand in mine, looking out beyond the edge of the cliff where the ground fell away in a sharp slope that jutted down to the beach below. The sun was bursting with color, and low in the sky, ready to dip into the sea. We stood there together for a long time, watching it plunge and fade away.

Each new moon I would wind my way around the hill and through the dense wood to the bustling town of Moana to trade for supplies. I used the name Juno, as I'd done when I'd met Zeus, under strict instruction from Hecate to hide my lineage. Hecate sent me with brewed herbs and distilled oils from our summer work, and I traded them with the women in the market. Everyone knew of the wise old woman on the hill, and they were eager to take her tinctures, and honor me as her niece, often insisting on giving me far more then I asked for in return. They took me in, kind and endearing, offering their homes and friendship. As the years passed, I spent many days and nights with them, learning their ways, and becoming as much a part of their community as I could, always careful to hide the truth.

With each visit, I'd learn the news that travelers and traders had brought with them as they passed through town. This is how I found out that the Emerald Temple had declared me deep in the mystic priestess practices, and would not confirm my location. Rumors had spread that I was sequestered in the actual temple itself as no one had seen me leave the isle. Others placed me across the sea in Malta, where the tribal priestesses of the Aegean gathered each year. There were even outlandish tales that imagined me catered to in dynastic estates across the northern mountains, groomed as a noblewoman. Nothing that I heard was remotely close to the truth of my life with Hecate. For though she taught me the mysteries and the healing ways of the priestess, my routine each day was predictably simple, and I lived as any hermit might, working the land, and caring for my teacher.

Of the mystic priestess arts, I learned more than I would have back at the Emerald Temple, for Hecate was keen on initiating me. She would take my hands in hers, and I would feel the life force move from her palms into my own, awakening something long buried, but familiar. When I was slow to see the colors around the physical form, she placed her hands on my cheeks, leaned toward me, resting her forehead on my forehead. Our brows met, and a great illumination filled my inner sight. After that my inner vision came strong and clear.

In time I could rest into the life force as my mother had once tried to teach me, surrendering to that immortal current. I learned to listen to it and did my best to speak from *its* wisdom. The art of calling forth the elements from this place of a merger with the invisible force came easily. I could summon the wind and call to the rain clouds. Plants and animals let me reach out from within the current, and later, *as* the current itself. I'd become a soft light brushing against their illuminations, and they would open themselves to me. What I had once called a mystery I soon came to know as a friend.

Pegasus had responded in the most beautiful way to this merging and would come whenever I reached out to him with my mind and heart. He was a great comfort and steadfast comrade as we roamed free on the high plateau. He would covet the spring and summer grasses, prancing and charging through the fields on his own. Each night he would return to me and settle in the small paddock that housed Hecate's pony and cart. I'd call out to him with the silent voice, and he would whinny and bray in reply.

Though I could manage the mystic feats when in a state of empty presence, I had great difficulty drawing on them when I was engaged with the matters of life and in the company of others. It was clear that this was not so with Hecate, who knew no separation between the visible and the invisible forms and languages. I longed to know such freedom, but my mind was still young and often rash, and my emotions still tempted me to circle and remain in the feelings of loneliness and longing. It did not matter that I knew such feelings, though very real at times, were a trap. It did not matter that I knew such emotions were to be met kindly, cared for, and then released back into the current of life. My mind would linger, and my heart would grow heavy, as the sharp, poignant longing that still coiled within me, would arise. The ease and grace of my life were still not enough for me. The old restlessness often stirred, but I did my best to stop letting it rule me. The only ability that stayed close to me was the skill to raise the fire, and this I used with great caution and respect.

And so time passed, and I learned the ways of the priestess. My heart opened and quieted. I stopped fighting against the tide of my life and instead, gave myself to it.

On the summer solstice, of my third year with Hecate, the dream of the blue-eyed man reappeared. When I opened my eyes, returning from the dream, my body trembled and perspiration lay wet on my skin. I pushed back the furs and sat up, recounting the dream quietly, but out loud, into the dark. Hecate slept on the other side of the cave. I spoke the dream aloud as she had taught me, putting the images into words as clearly as I could, letting the dream speak *through* me.

I had been on a ship, unlike anything I'd seen in the small ports of my village home or even the merchant vessels of Moana. The ship's hull was immense and covered with black pitch. There were close to fifty oars in the water, and they moved in time to the beat of a drum. The blue-eyed man stood tall in the prow, as sailors rushed about me to raise the big, square sail. The oarsmen stowed their oars and reclined on their benches, half dead from exhaustion. All eyes were on the man and his tall, muscled form, naked to the waist, his hair falling in long dark waves to his shoulders. He faced a receding line of gray clouds and lifted his hands above his head as if in salute, or prayer, and called out to the wind; he *knew* its secret name. I watched as his body softened and could see the moment his conscious awareness lifted up, and out of it. His hands blazed with light that moved upward toward the ominous vapors. The gray billowing clouds seemed to recede, as they perceived his essence and his grace. A breeze rose about us. Men locked eyes and smiled. The sail caught the wind and billowed so that the crest emblazoned there was now vivid: two dragons painted there, red and green entwined.

I opened my eyes when I'd finished reciting the dream, or maybe it was a vision, for it was that clear and vivid. To my surprise Hecate's was sitting beside me, a candle flickering between us.

"Did you see his face?" She asked.

I shook my head.

"Is he the same man you dreamt of years ago?"

"Yes. I'm sure of that."

My stomach ached, and my heart still beat hard in my chest. Panic welled up inside me. Hecate stared at me intently.

"Describe him to me."

I tried, but couldn't see the man's face clearly in any of the dreams, though I had a strong pull toward him and a sense of familiarity that never seemed to change.

"And you're certain you've never met him?"

I faltered for a moment. I hadn't thought of Zeus in years, but his image and the strong sensations of that afternoon I'd spent with him swept over me.

"I don't know," I said. "There was a time—"

I told her of my brief encounter with Zeus. Her eyes widened when I spoke his name.

"Zeus, son of Kronos, head of the Titan dynasty. Hera, are you sure?"

Again I nodded. "He was handsome and strong, and I was powerfully attracted, but there was something more there, I know there was," I finished.

Hecate remained silent for a long time. The candle flame cast a warm glow about her face. She looked out to the opening of the cave, where the first traces of sunrise could be seen. Rocking back on her feet, she stood and beckoned me to follow.

"Wash away the dream now, and prepare the fire," she said.

She moved toward the back of the cave with the candle, where her long desk sat, with its papyrus, and scrolls, splayed across the surface.

I pulled my cloak around my shoulders and walked to the indoor hearth. With a slow, deep breath, I moved my palm over the tinder. It crackled and leapt into flame. I stepped outside, the candle still lighting my way. Just below the entrance of the cave was the well. I let down the bucket, hauling up a fresh pail of water and returned to the cave. I glanced towards the back of the space where Hecate rummaged through scrolls, throwing open old trunks I'd never seen her touch before.

Continuing my morning rituals, I reached for a log and placed it on the fire, sending the smoke up and out the mouth of the cave. Then I filled the water pot and set it on the old stone in the middle of the hearth, pulling the morning herbs from my pocket. I laid them on the surface of the water, blessing my body and the day.

With the rest of the water, I washed, scrubbed my teeth with mint-leaf, and then poured the tea into two mugs. Again I looked towards the back of the cave, but still, Hecate hunted through her old papers, boxes, and scrolls.

The sun, which rose behind the hills, filled the sky with pale light. I laid sweet honey cakes on a plate and sat down by the fire waiting for her to join me. It was several more minutes before she moved to her place by my side, holding a piece of leather. There was a symbol engraved on its surface. She held it up before the fire so that the flames cast an orange and crimson hue across its surface.

"Is this what the dragons looked like?" she leaned close. "Be exact now, it matters. There are dragon symbols from the eastern tribes that are very different than the ones seen in Atlantis. Are these the dragons you saw?"

I stared at the darkened forms on the leather and nodded. Traces of green dye still clung to one dragon, and the other was painted in a faded red. Hecate pursed her lips and blew out her breath in a long, stream. She rolled up the hide.

"Royal lines," she murmured, reaching for her tea. She sipped it slowly. "This is the symbol of the Sacred Marriage, Hera," she said.

"The Sacred Marriage?"

I leaned toward her, but she took her time to answer.

"The *Heiros Gamos,* Hera, is a symbolic union of opposites—the union of sky and earth, of light and dark, feminine and masculine—to declare that our differences do not separate us from the one true force that unites us all."

Pulling up my knees I rested my head on my hands.

"I don't understand this concept called marriage. In the village of my childhood, women take mates, Hecate; they do not get *married.* There is no vow taken to another. How can anyone promise anything but love? What else endures? And this idea that one belongs to another, well, I don't understand how that can ever be so. There is no insistence on male and female unions. One looks for the spirit. There is no care for the body it is housed in."

"The Sacred Marriage is an ancient tradition brought forward in times of great peril," Hecate replied. "It is a union of the male and female aspects within any two people. The *Heiros Gamos* is a vow itself, you see, to unite for the benefit of all beings. It was a promise of balance and union, taken by the leaders of warring peoples, with the intention to bring peace to the land. The Heiros Gamos was not only a vow taken by men and women—any two people uniting for the benefit of all beings—that was its purpose." Hecate shook her head, throwing up her hands, "Now all that has been lost! The idea of it has been spread to the tribes on the mainland, by our priests, and from them, it has returned to Atlantis, but in a new form. It is no longer a sacred union, but a sort of contract of ownership and responsibility. The marriage is a union between a man and a woman, one that places the man before the woman. A union that is badly used and out of balance."

There was a deep look of sadness that came over Hecate's face. Her eyes seemed glazed as they rested on the flames.

"The women of the tribes go to marriage without choice. They have no say and no strength, or ability to resist. Some find caring, but most are badly used with little hope of discovering their true nature, or their vast ability for love."

The sky was now vibrant with color. Birdsong had risen outside. Chickens clucked to be freed from their pen. I looked out, past the fire, into the fresh morning. Concern over what seeing the symbol meant made me restless.

"Why would I see such a thing?" I asked, almost annoyed. "And why with such clarity of vision?"

Hecate shook her head.

"I cannot say why, but know this, Hera. It is because of the establishment of marriage that women are losing their power, dignity, and freedom all across the earth. As the concept spreads, it endangers the authority of the feminine face of the life force. No person should ever be held above another. No gender should be held in higher esteem!"

She almost spat these last words. Standing up she moved beside me and placed a gentle hand on my cheek.

"In a true Heiros Gamos, the union is pure, feminine and masculine standing together, equal and honored. If there was to be such a Sacred Marriage again on Atlantis, one sanctioned and respected by all; it might change the way marriages are perceived and entered into. A true Heiros Gamos might change the tide."

She patted my shoulder.

"Let it go now, child," she said. "Take Pegasus to the ocean and let the salt water clean away the worry between your brow!"

I smiled at the thought of it and reached out to Pegasus with my silent voice. I could hear his hooves on the turf outside as he moved toward the cave. The day was already warm, so I slipped on my sandals and dropped my cape. My hair was long and unbound, my skin tanned dark from long outings in the sea. It was the hottest spring we'd had since I'd been with Hecate and the air in the cave, though cooler than most places, was very still. It would be good to get outside to clear my mind and ease my feelings.

I reached for my pack and water bag, as I strode out of the cave to greet Pegasus. He trotted up to me and nuzzled me playfully. I ran my hand down the length of his neck and took hold of the coarse, white hair of his mane. I had no saddlecloth and vaulted easily onto his back. The muscles of his body gathered and pushed beneath my thighs as he took off over the hill and down the steep path toward the beach, where we could run free.

At the bottom of the trail was the sacred grove of Banyans, and we cantered around it in respect. When we reached the beach, Pegasus bolted free into the soft sand. I leaned into him, letting his powerful sounds thunder over me. The deep whistle of his breath over the crush of his hooves thrilled me. He ran with a fury toward the water. Gripping tighter with my legs, I braced as he lunged into the surf, white foam rising in the air to cool us both. I laughed. My body surged with his, and I leaned forward, urging Pegasus to go faster. As we rounded the bend on the beach, crossing below a large outcropping of black rocks, I sucked in my breath, suddenly sensing something ahead. Pegasus felt it too. He flattened his ears back, listening, and then pushed his head sharply forward. Feeling a change in his stride I tightened my grip, chiding myself for having no bridle. I wrapped the fingers of both hands tight into the long strands of his mane and braced myself as we came about the rocks.

Pegasus reared.

Every muscle in my body clutched at him, trying to stay astride. He came down hard, his hooves dashing at something before I could will him back. A large, black hound darted from beneath his stance, and then there was a yelp as another followed. Pegasus circled violently, his high-pitched scream matched by the ferocious baying of dogs, though they now stood back at a distance. As I reached out to Pegasus with my inner voice, calling him to settle, I looked up to see a small group of men standing before me, wide-eyed. They each held a weapon in their hands.

Two moved quickly, calling off their dogs, and another, a huge, fair-haired figure, stepped forward. He taunted me with his eyes, and though I could see that he didn't recognize me, I knew him at once as Ajax, Zeus's man. My skin prickled with warning.

I took the scene in quickly. Tents were still set up in the sand behind them, and a man stood by a fire pit, dousing it with sand. There were six altogether.

I whistled hard to get Pegasus's mind back on mine. He calmed as the dogs returned to their handlers, but he wouldn't settle at the sight of the swords. There was a sound from above us, and everyone turned, looking up at a man who stood on top of the rocky crest that overlooked the stretch of sand I'd just come from. He signaled to his fellows as he approached and they put up their swords. I steadied Pegasus as the man approached, a chill sweeping over my skin at the sound of his voice, even at a distance. His black hair was longer than I remembered it, and his skin dark brown from too much sun, but there was no mistaking who he was, and for the first time I thought I understood the reason for my dream.

CHAPTER TWO

ZEUS WAS DAZZLING. He bounded toward me; his blue eyes fixed on mine.

"It's you," he cried as I sat staring, my jaw wide-open. "Juno, come, we mean you no harm."

I slid from Pegasus's back and stood before him, signaling my stallion to withdraw a few paces. The men seemed immediately impressed with that, and they came toward me in a group, but Zeus waved them back. He came to me eagerly, snatching up my hands. I shifted uncomfortably as sensual warmth moved over me from his touch. I smiled despite myself.

"What are you doing here?" I asked, trying to take hold of my feelings.

"It's fate!" he cried.

He spoke quickly, gesturing to his companions, but I only half heard what he said as my eyes traced the pleasing line of his lips. They had just returned from Kart Hadst in the Mediterranean, where they'd brought shiploads of new settlers. They were recruiting again across Atlantis to fill their legions. He pointed to a thin, straight-nosed man, whom he introduced as Hades, his half-brother. Stepping forward,

Hades contorted his face into a half sneer as he eyed me. He was not as tall as Zeus, nor as sturdily built. His chin was covered with a dark beard, his clothes very fine, and he wore a somewhat imposing jewel-hilted sword at his waist.

Zeus signaled Ajax, who returned to the men, ordering them to strike down the tents. Hades remained by Zeus's side.

"I watched as you were riding from atop the stones," Zeus said, bringing my attention back to his gleaming eyes. "I've never seen a woman ride like that, and your horse, Juno, he's magnificent."

He looked toward Pegasus admiringly, and I grew warm with pride. Pegasus cantered about the beach, showing himself off. This set the dogs to baying once again. Even the other men hesitated in their work to watch his fine form on parade.

When I turned back to Zeus, he was staring at me. I could see the pleasure in his look, and despite myself, I blushed. He brushed my cheek and lowered his voice. "I looked for you."

"I was sent away, to serve," I replied.

He looked about quizzically.

"I serve the old woman on the hill," I murmured.

"The hag?" interjected Hades.

I gave him a hard look, offended by his words.

Zeus threw up his hands apologetically. "He didn't mean—" he started in a low tone.

"You defend my words, brother?" Hades said testily. "And to *this* woman?"

Zeus turned to him and said something I could not hear. It must have been harsh, for Hades lifted his brow and took a step back.

"My family owes the old woman a debt, and my service is payment," I said to Hades, my head held high. "It is an honorable trade."

Zeus turned back to me admiringly. "Well spoken, Juno."

Hades narrowed his eyes. "I see," he said. "So, you're a serving girl. Well, I suppose I should be used to that by now; my brother is served by so many women."

Zeus's cheeks flushed. He shut his eyes and bent his head as if searching for control of his temper. "Hades—" he began, but his brother continued in a derisive tone.

"Zeus, she's just another girl. We're late, and our father is waiting."

Zeus turned on him. "I will not be lectured to, brother!" he said. "And Juno isn't just a serving girl. I won't have you speak to her that way!"

I was startled by the intensity of his voice and the way he defended me. I could see that Hades was as well. He glanced from Zeus to me as if he was looking for something he'd missed. When he didn't find it, he lifted himself up and stepped forward stiffly.

"My apologies, brother," he said. "She is rather beautiful if you like a tribal face."

Zeus waved him away. "Collect the horses, Hades," he commanded. "I'll join you shortly."

Hades was obviously offended by the dismissal. I took a step closer to Zeus and placed my hand lightly on his muscled arm. Zeus relaxed and smiled down at me, then turned his back on his brother.

Hades placed his hand on the jeweled hilt of his sword, scowling. He shot me a hard look before he moved away toward the others.

"I'm sorry, Juno," Zeus said. "He's a priest," he added as if that explained his brother's behavior.

I nodded. "I've never met one before."

He laughed at that. "They're all the same," he said.

His riders mounted their horses and called to their dogs. Zeus glanced over his shoulder and then back to me.

"Look, Juno, I have to go, but my father has a house set up, for me, and my men, in Moana," he said, quickly. "We'll be using it as our base throughout the summer. We're scouting the west for recruits. I'll be here, and I want to see you."

I knew I should shake my head, to call to Pegasus and leave, and not look back, but I found myself reaching out a hand, regally, toward Zeus instead.

"I'll be here tomorrow," I said.

Zeus grinned. "As will I," he answered.

When I returned to the cave, Hecate was waiting by the well. The scrying bowl, a shallow, copper plate filled with water, was set out on a pedestal in the sun. Hecate used it for visioning. I'd thought on whether I should say anything, or not about Zeus, but it was apparent she already knew.

"At least I understand the dream, now," I said.

"Perhaps," she said evasively. "Time will tell."

"But surely, he's the man in the dream," I replied wanting more from her.

She sat there quietly and poured the water out of the bowl.

"The man in the dream symbolizes Zeus, right?" I pressed her. "And the ship must be a sign of his travels?"

Hecate picked up an old cloth and rubbed it gently over the copper surface.

"Some dreams are symbolic," she said, "while others are waking dreams and are true connections. Only you can say for sure which kind yours was."

"But Hecate," I said pacing uneasily, "To have the dream and then meet him here like this...what else could it mean?"

"Many things," she said.

I stopped moving, startled by her rapid reply.

She rose from her work and wrapped the sacred visioning bowl in its leather cloth.

"Trust yourself, Hera," she said. "That is all I have ever meant to teach you." With that she turned, and went back into the cave, leaving me with my uncertain feelings.

I turned to my work to calm myself. I pulled our pelts from the dark interior of the cave and laid them out in the open, beneath the sky. We would sleep outside all summer, listening to the night sounds and the crashing of the waves on the shore below. I set Pegasus to pasture and gathered wood and weeded the long rows of beans, but my mind kept returning to Zeus. The strong desire for my lover pushed away the subtle sense that something was wrong, out of place. By dusk, I'd stopped wondering what the dream meant and instead let my mind indulge in its obsession, visualizing Zeus's lips pressed against my own.

The next morning Hecate was nowhere to be seen. I searched the cave and the orchard and traveled up beyond the mango groves, but I could see no tracks on any trail she might have taken. So, I snatched my pack and filled it with kukui nuts and barley cakes and a small flask of wine I'd been given months back. I reached for a soft sheepskin blanket and called Pegasus to me, bringing a bridle and soft saddlecloth. Then I made my way down the path to the beach. It was still morning when we reached the place of the men's camp. I let Pegasus run free on the beach as I walked up behind the rocks and spied a small stretch of sand protected by the stones. The wind couldn't reach me here. I laid out the blanket and food, and then returned to the beach.

He was standing on the sand beside one of the large, jutting rocks, unbridling his horse, a stunning brown stallion with a white bolt across its brow. The horse bristled, shook his head and moved about, but didn't take off in its determined freedom as Pegasus had done. He eyed me uncertainly. He clearly would not leave Zeus's side.

Zeus turned and faced me. I smiled.

I reached out my hand and led him to our alcove behind the rocks.

CHAPTER THREE

WE MET ALMOST EVERY DAY throughout the late season and into the early fall. Zeus shirked his responsibilities as often as he could, and I made a sad attempt to honor my own. Hecate didn't chastise me or stop me from my affair. Since word had come that I'd return to the temple at winter solstice for my ordination and take my place in the community, I made the most of my freedom.

Throughout that time Zeus was much on my mind, and my body craved him in ways I'd never known before. When I was with Zeus, I could see that I'd changed a great deal in the years with Hecate. My outlook had become more moderate, and I was far less restless. I'd grown taller, my hips had flared into a feminine form, and my hair was thick with brown ringlets. My body had somehow deepened as if I held more in the hollow of my womb. I was aware of something softer, and profound, a desire that reached out to touch my lover and pull him in. Hidden needs revealed themselves, places that ached for touch and movement and sound. Supple and yielding, I'd learned to slow down and rest into the moment—the soft sand beneath me, my lover's body above. The sound of the sea, his breath, the arching up and pulling in.

On hot nights, I'd lie beneath the stars, sleepless, tracing our lovemaking in my mind. My body opened to him when we were together, and I found it longing for his touch when I was alone. When he'd travel to another town for days at a time, I wondered if he made love to other women, but the thought didn't disturb me so much as the idea of not getting to lie with him again myself.

Our natural passion formed a bond between us. I would not have called it love, but friendship born of caring and desire. I made great efforts to keep our conversations away from the Emerald Temple and my past with sensual offers of my body, for I knew I couldn't tell Zeus my true identity. Zeus also withheld things from me. He skillfully avoided sharing Titan affairs of state or the details of wars, which they called *expansion efforts*. In this way, we formed an alliance of sorts, one that had little to do with honesty, and things that have real heart and meaning. I indulged in the physical needs of my body, oblivious to the consequences, or the hand of destiny upon me, until one day, Zeus's desires changed, and the reality of our differences caught up with me.

It had been a long and sensuous morning, and we ran to the surf to relieve the heat, sliding into the cool water, our bodies gliding against each other in the shallows, like dolphins playing. He slid up behind me, one hand about my waist, the other cupping my breast, and kissed the salty skin of my shoulder.

"Juno, I must tell you, I've been with many women," he said suddenly.

I couldn't help but smile. "Yes," I said teasingly, "and I thank every one of them for what they've taught you!"

I moved easily about in his hands. The smooth caress of his chest against my breasts made me shudder. His feet were buried in the soft sand, anchoring us in place as the warm waves pulled gently at our bodies. I slid myself against him, moving toward his mouth for a kiss, but he stopped me.

"Doesn't that bother you?" he said. "The thought of me with others?"

My hands were about his neck, and he was holding me, rocking protectively in the gentle surf. I sensed the seriousness of his tone but wasn't sure how to answer.

"No," I replied honestly.

I reached up and stroked his face gently, willing my desire to soothe his unease. He relaxed beneath my touch and my lips, but when I pulled away his eyes were brooding.

"There's something about you," he went on, "Not just that you're beautiful, so many women are—"

I bit his chin, gently.

"Yes?" I said, absently, moving his hand to my breast.

"I miss you when I leave," he went on, "and I feel more of myself with you than anyone else, Juno. You've become like home to me."

I wrapped my legs about his waist and pressed my lips to his forehead. Placing my palms, strong and sure against his cheeks, I kissed him again. I held him in the water until both our bodies had puckered.

We laughed as we returned to the cove and lay in each other's arms while the sun baked us dry. The tall stones about us cast a shadow across half of Zeus's body as he lay beside me, but he didn't mind, as the day was hot. He shut his eyes, and I found my place in the crook of his arm, and immediately drifted into sleep. The waves on the shore lulled me as I shut my eyes. I knew I should be going that Hecate had things for me to do, but the moment was a languid one. *I'll just rest here for another moment,* I thought, and then I was asleep.

I was immediately in a dream. I stood in a field of golden wheat with the sun warm on my back. My grandmother and Artemis stood on the far side, waving. I moved toward them, slowly, the dream making every movement an exaggeration of time. Then I looked down and saw that I was naked. My breasts were larger, swollen, the skin around my enlarged nipples, dark. My belly was thick and round. I stopped. *I am with child,* I thought. Artemis called out my name, and when I looked up, she was holding a small girl on her hip, a broad smile on the child's face as she waved to me. *Mama,* she cried out, the sun giving her bronze hair an ethereal aura of gold. I heard my voice call her name: *Ilithyia.*

I awoke with a start, shaking hard. Quietly, I eased myself from Zeus's arm and fumbled for my tunic, slipping it over my head. I reached for my sandals as I called Pegasus with my mind. Before I slipped away, I turned to look at Zeus' beautiful body, still asleep. His hair was drying in curls about his cheeks, and his lips were slightly parted as he breathed. He looked vulnerable. I leaned down and kissed him gently on the forehead. He murmured my name and reached out, but I took up his hand in mine and laid it on his chest.

"Sleep now, love," I whispered close to his ear. "I have to go."

He pursed his lips and opened his eyes. "You can't go yet, Juno, I'll be traveling for a full turn of the moon," he said unhappily. "I need you."

I placed my hand on his cheek and kissed him long and full so that he reached for me again, but I only laughed and pulled away. He didn't laugh with me, but sat up on an elbow and held tight to my hand. He looked into my eyes, his heavy brows furrowed, chasing away the sweet, boyish look.

"I love you, Juno."

A shock ran through me. Uncomfortable, I pushed him away. "You've loved many women," I said.

"No, listen to me. When I'm with you, there is no other," he said.

"And when you're not?"

We both knew the answer, and it made no difference to me. I knew I didn't love him that way.

"We should marry!" he said.

I stiffened.

"Marriage means I'll be yours forever," he said as if that would please me. "I'll be your husband, and you'll be my wife. I'll provide you with a good home, Juno, here in Atlantis. In the new city of Kart Hadst we'll have an estate and our children will have prestige and power."

I shook my head, thinking of the dream child, sure that I carried her already. I pulled away from him instinctively, but he sat up and moved forward. He was obviously excited and had thought this through.

"There's so much I can give you, Juno, a life of finery. I've got wealth of my own, and we won't need to stay in my father's house or play their political games." He leaned in close and dropped his voice. "I'm the youngest son, but I have my prestige, my place outside their scheming. Juno, I've amassed and trained a deadly force of men, and it's growing every day. Do you understand what that means? Imagine, five thousand men that will strike on my word alone."

He smiled broadly as if he was offering me the world, and suddenly I realized that he was! I grew wary, and my stomach tightened. Trusting the reaction of my body, I reached out gently. "Zeus, this is not the path for me."

He raised his brows and let out a disgruntled breath.

"Juno," he continued, speaking slowly as if to make himself more clear. "I'm telling you that my star is rising and I want to take you with me! In a few more years I'll be one of the most powerful men in Atlantis, I swear it."

I looked at him anxiously. "Zeus, please, there are things you don't know about me, things I haven't told you and that you won't like."

He shook his head. "There's nothing I need to know, Juno. I want to marry you. I want you to be mine *forever.*"

A sickening feeling ran through me, and suddenly I remembered my last dream with the blue-eyed man. Hecate had said the symbol in my dream had something to do with a sacred marriage, but I did not consider anything Zeus was telling me to be holy. Again, my body lurched away.

Zeus grew agitated and retook my hands and kissed them. He pulled his heavy gold medallion from around his neck and pressed it into my palms.

"A sign of my pledge to you," he said. "Look, it is my insignia, the thunderbolt. One day, Juno, I will rule a dynasty of my own."

My mouth was dry and my throat tight. I felt his intense desire to...have me. I pushed the medallion back gently.

"Oh, Zeus," I said softly, as I pulled away and looked at him. "It's a wonderful offer, and I do care for you. But my life is set on a different course."

He looked as though I'd slapped him. His face changed, his tone became petulant.

"I don't understand!" he thundered. "How can you not consider these things an honorable way of life, a grand step in your circumstances? Marriage is the new way of building family, and I will make you rich, and give you a new station in life if you stand at my side."

I shook my head again. "I want nothing to do with such a thing as…marriage," I said, standing up and walking away. He leapt to his feet and stalked toward me, taking hold of my arm in a frantic gesture.

"Marriage is an absolute necessity. How can Atlanteans expand into tribal lands if we have no rules for their people to adopt? How will they respect us?"

I looked at him in disbelief.

"We have the old ways, Zeus. Why shouldn't they respect our traditions of equality and mutual understanding?" I demanded. "Why should a woman attach herself to one man, when surely a man will not attach himself to one woman?"

He threw up his hands and lifted his brow as if the answer was obvious.

"A woman must be faithful to a man, Juno, or how will he know if her child is his?" He took up both of my hands as if speaking to a young child. "Try to understand that the old ways are broken. Men are gaining power and fortune. Dynasties are enduring for generations. Men and women must come together for more than pleasure. They must build something, something great and enduring, a family that is structured, a lineage that grows in power over time. A man must have a son that will carry his name after he is gone."

I was stunned into silence. Pegasus paced before our alcove, and I could hear the soft huff of his breath as if he was outraged as well.

So, this is what it all came down to. A man must have a son to pass his life over to. I saw that Zeus had no real inkling of what he was saying. The truth that he was trying to create a way to live on after death, through his son, and his son's sons, completely eluded him.

I turned to go shaking off Zeus's hand as he tried to stop me.

"Juno, I offer you another way of life," he insisted, following me outside the cove.

A cool breeze rose off the white-capped water before us. I reached for a leather cord to bind back my hair, trying to ignore him. He stamped hotly into to the space between Pegasus and me.

"My family wants me to marry a woman from one of the great houses. That's what I should do, Juno, to help myself take power more easily. But I'm willing to give that up for you!" he shouted.

I stepped back, looking up into his furious face, incredulous.

"I'm the youngest son," he went on, "and yet the most mighty in my father's house. Men follow me, Juno. I have power and prestige, but no title. I can seize one through marriage and rise above my brother's and my circumstance! I'm willing to give that all away for *you!*"

"I'm not asking you to!" I snapped.

His face grew hard and cold. He clenched his fists at his side and set his lips hard against each other.

"Then there's no point in our seeing each other," he exclaimed.

"Fine!" I replied.

He turned his back to me abruptly and moved up the steep, weeded slope to the plateau above where his horse waited. When he got to the top, he stopped. I could feel his urge to turn around, and my desire to call out his name, but my pride and fear kept me silent. In a moment, he was gone.

CHAPTER FOUR

ILITHYIA.

A sense of beauty and softness welled up inside me as I let the name move up from my womb, brushing my lips like feathers. I would say her name out loud and revel in it, as I moved through my duties each day. Fetching water from the well, I'd dip my hand beneath the cold surface and whisper it, *Ilithyia.* The sound pressed against the ripples and the dim outline of a child's face appeared, round and dimpled with pale shining blue eyes like her father's. There were times I missed Zeus and nights when I wished for his hand, warm on my skin, or his voice to comfort me. As the months passed and my stomach grew rounder, the desire for him lessened, as the new sensations and intuitions with my child delighted me.

I began to sew. I made warm boots out of the softest deer hide, and an exquisite linen gown with embroidered sleeves. I sketched a pattern of the dragon on the hemline and sang as I worked by the fire. Hecate flattered me, and plied me with herbs, lying her hands on my belly each day to send the sacred light of the priestess' love, blessing to the child's essence.

When I was five months gone, she sent word to the temple and had me write a private note to my parents. I knew that they'd be there for my ordination and that Artemis had long ago agreed to escort me to it, but I was more thrilled about my pregnancy then I could ever be about the ordination. I imagined Mother's smile when she unfurled the scroll, and Father's delight. Surely, they would now be at peace with the decision they'd made to send me to the temple. My life was on its right course.

Near the end of winter, a half moon after the news had been sent, Athena arrived, from the temple. Her horse gave a sharp cry, and Pegasus answered, alerting us to her presence. It was dusk and the fire lit. I sat over a large pot of stew, stirring in fresh onions, parsley, and thyme, breathing in their healing aroma, when I heard her footsteps on the path to the cave. I pulled myself up as she approached. My belly was now plainly visible even beneath my long robe, and I was so proud of the life I carried within it, that I smoothed the cloth of my tunic so that Athena would see.

Hecate greeted Athena at the mouth of the cave and Athena dropped to her knees out of formality. I had lived so long in the familiar company of my teacher that I often felt a shock at the stiffness and protocol of the temple ways.

When Athena got to her feet, she turned to me, eyeing my supple form. I smiled broadly, looking down at my belly then back to her expectantly, but she only nodded.

"So, I see it's true. You look well, Hera. Pregnancy becomes you."

I wanted to hug her, to lift her wonderful wizened hands and place them on my stomach, but instead, I bowed politely, offering my respects and turned back to supper.

Hecate and Athena sat down on the well-worn logs we

used as benches placed by the hearth. I dished out full bowls, and wooden spoons to each then took one for myself and listened to them talk.

"The High Priestess is pleased," Athena began. "She will have us keep the pregnancy a secret until Hera gives birth, and the child is pronounced healthy."

"A wise plan," Hecate said.

Athena nodded. "There has been much discussion about how to proceed, but before we can make any real plans, we must know one thing."

She paused and looked at me expectantly. I smiled and put my hand on my belly.

"I will have a daughter," I said.

Athena nodded, finally smiling. "Good," she said.

Hecate urged us to eat and pulled out a small flask of wine and mugs, offering Athena a draught.

"It's a long way to come," she said to Athena, "for such a simple answer. I wonder why the High Priestess did not sense this herself?"

Athena sipped the wine. "She has to be sure," she answered. "The Temple is under great scrutiny from the council at Caledocean. The Titan dynasty has taken more control and one of Kronos's sons, Hades, has made a play for power. The High Priestess cannot misstep now. She sent me because she *must* be certain."

I stirred the fire with a stick, my body tensing with the news.

"But how can they take more power?" Hecate hissed. "Politics and men, when will they ever have enough?"

Athena put down the mug and held her hands out to the flames.

"There are so many ways the priests are taking power, Hecate. I fear for our future."

The two women sat in silence for a while, and I cleaned away the supper. I went to the well and drew a fresh pail of water, and heard them laughing in the cave, which put me more at ease. When I returned, they had moved to the sitting rugs with their warm sheepskins and woolen blankets.

I sat down beside Hecate and pulled one around me, then reached for an oil lamp, but the flint was on the other side of the hearth. My body was tired and my belly, heavy. I reached out my hand instinctively to call the fire to light it when I heard Hecate's stern voice.

"No, Hera!" She moved quickly to my side. "Remember, you must never call the fire with a child in your body!"

Athena reached for the flint and lit the lamp, and two candles beside it. I glanced at her sheepishly.

"I'm sorry," I said, "I'm just tired, I forgot—"

"You can't afford to forget, Hera." Athena's look was severe. "Using any of your skills will affect the baby. You share the same resources, the same current. You must protect your daughter at all costs."

I nodded, color rising to my cheeks. "Of course," I said feeling foolish.

No matter how much time passed, I still felt small in Athena's presence.

Leaning back into the rugs, I tried to calm myself, and listen to their news.

"What of the tribes?" Hecate asked.

"It is a terrible time for the tribes," Athena began. "There is discontent brewing at the port of Kart Hadst on the mainland. It is our greatest port, and the best place to evacuate to, but it is controlled by warriors rather than leaders."

"Warriors?" Hecate questioned.

"The canal has been built by the tribes, but it is our

warriors that have persuaded them to do so. The town has grown into a small city, ruled by men with swords."

"What happened to the temples?"

"Overrun!" Athena put her hands on the sides of her head and exhaled heavily. I had never seen her so heavy of heart, nor did I realize how political her position was. My time at the temple had been one of training and immersion into temple life. I had not thought beyond that, to the responsibilities of a High Priestess and her dedication to protecting her people.

"We still have a small group of priestess' there, but they are housed in the lower quarters of the captain's quarters. And the priests, of course, have held on to their temple by force. This is how the Titan's have risen. One son leads the army, while the other leads the priests. A deadly combination."

"So, there are no women on the council of our new city on the mainland? It is only men that plan the expansion efforts there?"

Athena nodded and sat back. "The High Priestess has sent an emissary, but we have not heard from her as yet. The men push farther inland, taking the tribe's sacred land, and resources. It is only a matter of time until the tribes rise against us. We have taken what is rightfully theirs. I cannot blame them for their discontent."

Hecate bowed her head, "I've been dreaming it for quite some time, but the fighting is yet a ways off. And things will change, Athena. All is not lost. There are good men too, men who will defend what is right, and stand against their brothers until justice reigns."

Her words filled the cave with a palpable light. Athena sighed and her body visibly relaxed as if on Hecate's word alone, she could now put it out of her mind.

They talked late into the night, and at some point, I rose and went to my sleeping mat lulled to sleep by the hush of their familiar voices and laughter.

In the morning Athena supplied her packs and filled her water skins from the well. We walked her to the stable where she brought out a horse that was not her own. She did this each time she came so as not to be recognized in her travels. As she laid the saddle blanket over her mount, she spoke without looking at me.

"And the father, Hera?" she said.

I stepped back in surprise, looking to Hecate, but she only handed Athena the bridle.

"He's gone," I said.

Athena moved past me without looking into my eyes and slipped the bridle easily over her mare's high head. She laid the reins about her neck and turned to me.

"But who is he, Hera?" she said staring at me hard.

I swallowed, thinking what to say. "She was made with love, what else matters?"

Athena shook her head, unsatisfied. Gazing into my eyes, she seemed to soften. She reached out a hand to my cheek.

"Your grandmother will want to know," she said in a low voice.

She turned back to her horse and mounted. Lifting her hand, she waved farewell as she moved toward the trail and out of sight.

That night I lay awake a long time wondering what I would say when my grandmother faced me with the question herself. I couldn't think what difference it would make who the father was, except for the growing tensions between the house of Titan and the temple itself. An uneasy feeling came over me, and I slept restlessly. This went on for days, with Hecate making me herbs and draughts, but my mind would not ease. I turned to the sacred practices of chanting and the walking prayer to free myself of worry but found no peace. At night, when I did sleep, I dreamt badly. The old dream would come to me, the man shrouded in mist, the waves high on the sea, and now, each time I moved away from it, the sail of the ship flashed before me and the words lingered in my ears, *Heiros Gamos, Heiros Gamos.*

As winter came to a close, I grew hopeful that my mood would change for Artemis would soon arrive to take me to my ordination. I watched for her every day with increasing anticipation. She'd never been to Hecate's cave, which was hidden from the coast by thick, overgrown trails and forest. It was not an easy place to find, but Hecate reassured me.

"That one will ask the birds," she said, chuckling.

As Hecate had said, Artemis found her way easily, sending a flock of black winged birds to circle our cave before she stepped out of the woods silently before us. I dropped my sewing and stood, awkwardly heavy with child, reaching out to the air as if it would help propel me toward her. In a moment I was wrapped in her arms, her long hair about me and the familiar scent of coconut oil rising from her skin. I cried softly as she pulled away and held me from her, looking me up and down. I'd grown taller since we'd last met. My eyes now looked directly into hers, and my shoulders matched hers in height.

"You're even more beautiful, Hera," she said, wiping away my tears.

She pulled me to her again, and we embraced and

admired each other until we were both laughing as if no time had passed at all.

I took her hand and led her to the cave, leaving her pack by the trees. Artemis moved toward Hecate with ease.

"An honor to meet you, Reverence," Artemis said looking down into her eyes.

Hecate reached a hand to my friend's cheek. "No, daughter," Hecate responded, "time will show you that the honor is mine."

It was an unusual thing to say, and I noted the color rise to Artemis's cheek where Hecate had brushed it. She looked at me quickly, but I only shrugged and ushered her into a seat on the skins.

I made Artemis talk, happy just to hear the sound of her voice. My body responded as it always had, to the warm affection that filled her tone. She gave me all the news of our village. She told me how her grandfather had passed on, and that she had taken up his spear and now led the hunters in the old way. She spoke slowly and deliberately, her eyes bright. Oh, how I'd missed Artemis's eyes! I watched her full lips move as she spoke and I smiled with helpless desire as she reached out and squeezed my hand.

"Apollo has taken to the sea, serving as healer, on a vessel that is exploring the Aegean. The last I saw him he was very happy." She reached into a small bag that was tied to her belt and handed me a stone he'd wanted me to have. "He said it's very rare."

I turned the purple stone over in my palm and shut my eyes, sensing into it.

Warm. Content. Safe.

I opened my eyes delighted. Artemis was watching me, her brows raised.

"That's just how Apollo speaks to it," she said. She reached out a hand and brushed a loose strand of hair from my cheek. "You're a priestess already."

We sat without speaking for a few minutes, and I sipped my tea.

"Your mother has become a well-known healer," she went on. "People travel from all over the eastern shore to see her."

"And Father?"

She smiled and shook her head. "He's the same, Hera. He stays close to his fields, but the villagers honor him at every festival, and he always attends. He seems content. Your parents are looking forward to the ordination."

I shivered at that, realizing the time was coming so close now. There was no turning back, even if I'd wanted to. She noticed my agitation and reached out, but I shook her away and smiled.

"It's nothing," I assured her. "There's just so much to think about with the baby coming."

Artemis put her hand gently on my stomach then and leaned down to kiss it as if she couldn't help herself.

"A girl," she said warmly. "Oh, Hera, it's wonderful. You're going to have a girl!"

I moved closer to her and laid my head on her shoulder as I used to do. For the first time in many months, I felt safe.

We ate and drank. Artemis brought in her pack and pulled out a warm, black cloak that Mother had made for my ordination. I ran my hands over the finely woven thread, letting my fingers play over the embroidered symbol along the hem. The image of a serpent with a dragon's head at either side of the opening was needled in a crisp, intricate pattern of green thread. A new belt went with it and a beautiful brooch with the dragon inlaid in jade against a smooth, ivory background. It was placed in a hammered, bronze setting. *So,* I thought, *they will acknowledge my lineage at my ordination.* No one had mentioned this to me, and yet Mother knew already, or how could she have made these things? I wondered what else I was not being told. That strange anxiety moved inside me again.

I folded the items and put them away as Artemis washed and changed. Hecate pulled the flap of thick skins over the cave entrance, and the light of the candles flickered about the tall, black walls, while the sweet aroma of the beeswax softened my senses. I pulled Artemis to my sleeping furs and settled in beside her, draping her long arm over my body so that her hand rested on my stomach. I took a long, deep breath and shut my eyes, drifting easily to sleep.

The next morning was to be my last with Hecate. I spent it packing my things. Hecate added papyrus scrolls for my grandmother and bags of herbs while Artemis slipped down the hill and returned before the sun was full above us with a small shift pulled by two old mares. I marched out to the little cart, its two wheels hammered with bronze about the wood, and the small bed behind it filled with fresh, soft hay. I shook my head adamantly, knowing Artemis's intent.

"You're too far-gone, Hera," she said. "It's not safe for you to be riding Pegasus." She glanced at my belly with a slight grin. "I don't even think we could get you on him."

Hecate chuckled from her place by the chickens who scratched her feet looking for meal. I shook my head again, but Artemis moved past me as if I didn't exist. She reached for both our packs by the door and lifted them into the little cart. Then she and Hecate disappeared together into the cave and when they reappeared they each held a soft fur and laid these in the cart between the packs. I threw up my hands in a rage and stomped back and forth before the buggy as if I was a child, but neither woman heeded me. They continued with their plans, Hecate bringing gourds of water and Artemis tying a small goat behind the rig.

"It's a cart for farmers," I protested. "Or for hauling grain!"

Hecate handed Artemis a small sack of coins and bade her hide them well inside her cloak. "Stay at small inns and stables as often as you can, and keep her warm," she instructed as if I wasn't there and listening. "And do not let her walk too long without water and her herbs. She must not press this child too hard."

My temper calmed at her words. She reached up her hands to my cheeks. "Remember, Hera, what *you* feel, the *child* feels. Keep her safe."

I placed a hand over hers and relaxed. Tears came unbidden as I leaned down and hugged her soft frame, inhaling the familiar scents of wild herbs thick in her hair and on her skin.

Hecate's voice came low in my ear, in a gentle, soothing tone. "Remember, my daughter, that every life has meaning. The life lived most simply and without production is no more, or less, than the life lived as a queen."

They were odd parting words, but I took them in and kissed her cheek.

"I'll remember," I said hoarsely, "everything you've taught me."

We held each other for a long time, and she let me weep. When I quieted, she stepped away. I dried my cheeks with the back of my hand like a child.

Looking about our little clearing before the cave, I took in the simple scene one last time. The rooster scattered the hens as always. I felt the deep womblike pull of the cave and listened as the breeze rustled against the door skins that covered the entrance. Hecate reached out her hand, and Medusa slid from her arm onto my wrist.

I climbed into the cart, leaning back into the pile of furs. The air was cold, and I wrapped them gratefully about my shoulders. Artemis took hold of the mare's lead, moving down the path, away from the cave. Hecate stood at the mouth of the clearing, waving, and smiling broadly until we were out of sight.

This is how I began my journey back to the Emerald Temple.

CHAPTER FIVE

WE TRAVELED ALONG THE PATH by the sea most of the day until we came to Moana. There, we lodged with a woman I often traded with. She lived simply and gave us a warm bed for the night. I told her Artemis was my sister, come to bring me home for my labor. That was the story we told at each inn, and to the kind folk who took us in along the way.

I walked long stretches of dry road but was glad for the cart more often as not. The baby was restless inside me as we traveled as if she longed already to be free and walking at our sides. I became increasingly more uncomfortable with the weight of my body, having now passed my seventh full moon, and looked forward to the simple pleasures of the bathhouse once we reached the temple.

We left the shoreline and moved inland, traveling upon a fine, well-made road. The weather was unusually sharp and cold. At night, I could see the warm steam of my breath, and by day, I wrapped myself in a cocoon with the furs. Artemis led the way traveling in silence, leaving me to lean back in the hay and watch the clouds pass above me as we went. I dozed often and sometimes dreamt: the sea, a ship, the man in the mist and the dragons entwined....

As we drew closer to the temple, I began to recognize the vast green pastures and forested hills. When I caught sight of the first ring of standing stones, I felt a shiver run over my flesh. It was almost night, and in the growing darkness, the wild vitality of the place shone about it like a light from within.

As we passed the first circle, the stones seemed to reach out to me, and my child. The baby moved within me. Above my head, wings beat suddenly, and a flock of black birds dipped down, swooping about us. They were ravens, dark and sleek, cawing their blessings from the unseen realms. Artemis stopped the cart, and we watched as they circled three times then lifted up into the growing night.

"A sign that the ancestors are with us," I said.

She nodded, but her look was tense. "May it be so," she said.

Artemis led us another half mile before she stopped the cart and set up camp beneath a thick cover of trees.

"I smell rain," she said, unhitching the mares.

We slept lightly, as the rain beat against the tent through the night. At dawn, we rose, cold and stiff, stepping out into the dew-covered green. I looked about me recognizing the lower reaches of the valley.

"We're very close now," I said as Artemis pulled bread and cheese from her pack.

"We'll make good time if we break camp now. Are you rested enough?" she asked.

I arched my back, placing my hand on my belly. "I don't think it much matters when we leave, this little girl hasn't been still all night."

I couldn't help but smile at the thought of my baby, my little girl. When I looked up, Artemis was smiling as well.

Looking out over the valley I pointed to the place in the distance where the oaks and chestnuts crowded close, fighting for the light. Just beyond that thick grove, the holly trees glinted darkly against the dawn sky. That was where the road to the Emerald Temple lay. Big, dark clouds loomed in the distance.

We took down our camp and packed the little cart, but the sound of thunder rumbled up over the valley. It was strange weather for this time of year, and Artemis looked uneasy. She called in the horses and set us moving back on the road.

I traced the landscape as we went, and a few minutes into the journey, I recognized the tree line and the curve of the river ahead. A thin layer of mist rose from the earth about us.

I knew we were close to the lake.

Calling for Artemis to stop I got down from the cart and came to stand beside her. She shook her head looking at the sky in before us.

"I don't think we'll make it to the temple today," she said. "They are expecting us at the main gate and will have a priestess there to guide us over the land-bridge to the isle, but its too far to go in this weather."

"Yes," I agreed. There was a dull ache in my head from the cold weather and sleepless night. "Let us take another route," I said.

She looked surprised.

"You mean the lake?" she said.

I nodded. I could feel the water was close. We were on the Southern shore, where my mother had taken me so long ago, to the little boats that priestesses used to cross the lake.

I had a strong desire to see it suddenly, to set my feet upon the sand and let the heart of the temple call to me across the water. Artemis looked doubtful.

"We won't be able to raise the mist," she objected. "We are expected by the land bridge to the north."

I looked up at the sky and shook my head.

"We won't make it before the rain comes. There's a small shelter on the southern shore, where the boat keeper lives in the summer. We can make camp there until this weather turns." I looked at her pleadingly. "I'm tired, Artemis, and the child won't be still."

I placed my hands on my belly. A small pain stabbed there and down my legs. I needed to stretch. Artemis moved beside me and massaged my lower back and hips. Her hands were firm and slow, working expertly over the tender places and holding firm on the ones that ached. She pulled out a liniment and insisted I let her smooth it across my stomach as Hecate had shown her. I smiled as she fussed over me, but the cramps in my limbs didn't ease.

"Alright," she agreed, as another clap of thunder echoed through the valley.

She helped me into the cart. I lay back in the furs, but couldn't get comfortable, fidgeting as we left the road and headed out across the field toward the lake. We rode through fields of bluebells glossy and green, and the yellow-thorn was budding. Light showers fell upon us as we went, matting strands of hair to my face and misting my cheeks. Somewhere, sheep were crying.

I knew we should be moving faster, but the cart heaved back and forth uncomfortably about me even at a slow pace. Artemis would not push the horses afraid she would cause me pain. When finally we came over the ridge that looked down upon the lake and the crescent beach below, I slid out of the furs and onto my feet gratefully. Shaking my cloak free of moisture, I took up Artemis's hand and pointed to the small stone building just below us and to the trail that led around the bluff to the beach. She let the mares run free in the field, and then hoisted a pack to her shoulders. We headed down the rocky path.

The wind blew low and steady, sending dust and sand about us as we went along the narrow path. Artemis reached back for my hand through the descent, and I tottered down behind her. When we arrived the bottom, I told her to go on to the hut and start a fire in the hearth while I rested on a stone at the base of the hill.

"It's not far now," she said, "I'll wait with you."

"No," my voice was irritable. I was cold and hungry too. "Please, Artemis, let me rest here while you make the fire."

She shifted on her feet and looked down the beach at the cottage. I knew she didn't want to leave me, but I would be in sight. I pulled off the vial of medicinal oil, anointing myself with it, hoping the lavender and lemongrass would ease my mood.

Artemis pulled her cloak from her shoulders and put it around me.

"I'll get the fire started and then head back to help you the rest of the way. Don't push yourself, Hera. You look pale, and you need rest."

"Yes, you're right, I know."

She started off down the beach, picking up driftwood as she went. It didn't take long for her to reach the door and disappear inside.

Perched at the edge of the beach were the small crafts used to cross the lake. I remembered the way my mother had called to Demeter with her mind from the shore before we arrived the first time. If only Demeter would come now and lift the mist for us, we could be sleeping in soft beds at the temple before dark.

I shut my eyes then and let my mind picture Demeter, her broad, round face and earthy manner. I called to her, hopeful, across the water and beyond the temple walls that lay on the isle in middle of the lake. I imagined Demeter raising the mist, as a young priestess pulled at the oars, guiding their boat to shore. I fantasized her landing on the beach, her arms open to me in her warm and welcoming way.

When I opened my eyes, I shivered but smiled. I was so cold now anything was worth trying.

The baby stirred. I took a drink of water from my flask, and Medusa shifted about my neck. I thought to lie down in the sand to wait when I heard a strange sound. It was just a rustling at first and then the distinct sound of rippling water rising through the mist that hung heavy over the lake. I looked toward the water, and to my surprise, the mist thinned and lifted, the sound growing closer. For a moment I was disoriented, knowing that although this place made my abilities strong, Demeter had probably not received my summons and even if she had there was no way she could have crossed in such a short time. My eyes were riveted to the lake, and I stood, moving slightly behind the tall rocks that jutted out at the base of the trail, protecting myself from whatever came toward me on the water.

It was a small boat with a slight, cloaked figure pulling on the oars as it emerged from the gray wall of mist. I heard another sound further down the shore. From around the bend appeared two finely dressed men in the distance, moving toward the water. They both wore swords at their sides.

The taller one threw his cloak and sword belt to the sand splashing into the lake up to his knees, grabbing hold of the prow. He hauled it onto the shore. There, the other man held out a hand to the woman and eased her over the side onto dry land. Two bags were hauled out from inside, and then the tall man took up his blade and walked in my direction. I realized they were heading for the path Artemis, and I had just descended, and they were not aware of our arrival. I sat slightly hidden by a cone of rocks that jutted between us, but in a moment they would be upon me.

I looked down the shore realizing they had been waiting for this woman to come. And any woman coming across the water from the temple had to be able to raise the mist, or she'd be lost forever in the current of the lake. The only women who could do such a thing were highly trained priestesses.

Pulling myself closer to the stones I watched as the woman moved quickly toward the smaller of the two men and into his arms. They kissed deeply, and her hood fell back from her face. I squinted between the rocks to see, but couldn't make out her features. Their voices carried on the wind as they turned and moved toward me. I heard the woman laughing. I caught my breath and stepped back deliberately behind the rock.

The woman was Persephone.

My mind raced as I realized what I was witnessing. Persephone was my friend. She had always been my ally at the temple. She had taught me so many things and welcomed me as a sister. I was responsible for her as she was for me. I breathed hard and a sharp pain shot through my chest. The baby kicked, and I tensed my body.

The voices drew closer, and I thought of Demeter and what she would do when she found her daughter had broken her vows and...*and what?* Pressing myself against the rocks, I crouched down, watching as she approached. She was happy, smiling broadly, her small face looking adoringly up into the face of her lover.

I froze.

I knew that face, those cold, heavy-lidded eyes and that slight sneer of a mouth.

Hades.

A few paces behind, carrying Persephone's packs, strode Zeus.

I struggled to my feet, trying to think, but hard sound of heavy footsteps rose behind me, and I turned to see Artemis thundering down the trail. Stepping toward her hesitantly, I reached out my hand, but she had apparently seen the trio for she had her blade in her hand. As the three stepped around the rocks, the sun broke through the clouds, and the flash of her blade caught the dappled streaks of light.

Hades pulled Persephone behind him, and Zeus dropped the packs, reaching for his sword. I heard myself shout, and threw up my hands to stop him, but a pain seized my belly so sharply that I stumbled and fell to my knees, gasping for breath. Zeus froze midway toward Artemis, staring at me in shock.

"Juno," he said, "Juno what—?"

He stepped toward me, but Artemis hurled her body between us, her blade biting at his throat. Zeus lifted his weapon in a defensive posture.

"Who are you?" Artemis challenged.

"I'm a Titan," Zeus retorted.

I pulled myself back to my feet, throwing up my hands again.

"It's alright, Artemis," I said breathlessly, "I know him." I looked back and forth between them. "I know them all," I finished.

Persephone stood motionless at Hades' side, gripping his arm tightly. Her eyes seemed to plead with me, dismay plain on her face. Artemis still stood between us, her blade in her hand pointed at Zeus whose face had clouded with anger. I reached for her hand and pushed the blade aside, beckoning her to put it away, but as I stepped forward, another pain seized me, and this one wrapped so tight about my belly that my knees buckled beneath me. Artemis caught my arm, and Zeus lunged for my other, and between them, they eased me back to the sitting stone beside the rocks, out of the wind. Persephone left Hades' side and rushed to my aid. She took up my hand and felt for my pulse as Zeus stared wide-eyed at my belly.

"You're pregnant?"

I nodded, sucked in my breath, and squeezed his hand as another pain cracked across my abdomen like lightning.

"I'm sorry," I said, gasping. "I should have told you, and I would have, but—"

I couldn't finish. Sweat broke across my forehead, and the pain gripped my ribs and chest. I struggled to keep my breathing even. Persephone turned to Hades and called for her bag.

"Did you bring herbs?" she asked Artemis. Artemis nodded but hesitated. She would not let go of my hand or leave me alone with these people. Anxiety was etched across her face.

"It's alright, Artemis, I tell you I know them."

"But I don't," she said.

Persephone pulled the vial from about her neck and cracked it open. A strong, sweet scent rose in the air. She bathed my forehead in it and directed me to breathe it in. After a moment, the pain quieted and I could sit up straight again. I let go of Zeus's hand and turned toward Artemis.

"This is Zeus," I said quietly. "He is the father of my child."

Persephone gasped, and Hades stepped forward. Zeus reached for my hand again, but I didn't take my eyes from Artemis. Her look hardened for a moment and she took a deep breath, and something sad passed between us. Then she let go of my hand and nodded.

"I'll get your herbs," she said, turning toward the cottage in the distance.

Another pain gripped me as I watched her go. It was an intense contraction, followed by another and I looked helplessly toward Persephone who shook her head.

"Zeus lay out your cloak and help make her more comfortable," she said. He did as she directed, then reached for his water bag and tried to have me sip some, but the pains came again, one upon the other so that I could hardly catch my breath. I cried out, and he took my hand, his eyes filled with concern.

"Juno," he said again and again, "I'm here, my love, it's going to be alright."

Persephone and Zeus tried to move me, to take me to the cottage, but my body contorted and I cried out. Zeus eased me back to the sand, wrapping me in his arms. His hands were slick with sweat, and his breath was audible. Concern was evident in his voice as he called to his brother to take my other arm so that they could carry me between them, but as Hades approached Medusa slithered up from beneath my collar and hissed at him. Zeus cursed, falling backward as he reached for his knife to slice her away from me, but I shrieked, and Persephone grabbed his wrist.

"She belongs to Hera!" she cried, pushing her body between us. "Medusa's sacred to us, put up your blade."

There was confidence in Persephone's voice that surprised and relieved me.

Hades stood several steps away, but he moved towards us then, his eyes wide.

"*Hera?*" he said, his voice low and sharp. "Did you call her Hera?"

Persephone fell back to her place before me, waving him away. She wiped her forehead with the back of her sleeve and poured more oil into her hand.

Zeus reached for my hand again but stared at me hard.

I looked behind me, relieved to see Artemis jog toward us with the bag. She sat down beside Persephone to sift through the herbs. I reached for Artemis's hand.

"Medusa," I gasped, and she nodded, guiding the snake to slide from my neck, down my arm onto hers. For a moment our hands were bound by the strong folds of the snake's coils, and a chill moved over my skin. The contractions quieted for a moment and let me breathe as I looked into my friend's eyes. She returned the look, as Medusa slithered about her shoulders.

Then I screamed.

The pain rose up so sharp and sudden that the sound shrilled about me before I knew it was my voice. I grasped my waist and shook. It felt as though the child pressed herself into my spine. Hands were on me again, and I heard Zeus's voice commanding Hades help. I struggled to open my eyes, seeing Artemis's worried face, and Persephone's dark eyes darting frantically between us.

"The child's coming," she said.

"It's too soon," Artemis countered. She turned to Persephone with a desperate look, "You're a priestess. You can do something!"

Another wrenching pain struck me, and I cried out. I gripped Zeus's hand desperately.

Persephone moved behind me, running her fingers up and down my spine, pressing firmly. The pain eased, and I gasped again for breath. She held me in her arms for a few minutes, her voice kind and lulling as she tried to guide me to a peaceful state, but I could sense my daughter's hands inside me pressing to be free. I shook my head. *No, it's not time, Ilithyia.*

Another spasm sucked away my breath. I felt Artemis hold my head as I leaned forward on my knees, and heard Zeus's voice helplessly murmuring my name. When the spasm lessened, Persephone was on her feet.

"I can't stop this," she said, "we have to get her back to the temple where my mother can lay hands on her, and there isn't much time."

"The boat!" Zeus cried letting go of my hand and leaping to his feet. "Hades, help me."

He reached down to lift me to my feet, but Hades didn't move.

"We can't send Persephone back there now," he said sharply.

Zeus swore. He reached for his brother's arm and swung him about, hard, to face him, but Hades stood his ground.

I closed my eyes, pain, and confusion all about me. I tried to rest inside myself, to shut them out, and find an inner passage to a visual light, the representation of the life current. I heard their voices rise and then hands were upon me as they tried to lift me. My voice came out weak and wavering.

"I can't, the baby—" I was sobbing.

My voice seemed far away, and I was lost again in the pain as they set me back down. Time passed, and their voices merged, as I was lost in waves of shocking pain. Finally, I felt faint, and my awareness lifted up toward a vast, empty place. I heard Artemis's desperate plea, "Hera!" and felt her hand gripping me hard, but I was moving fast toward unconsciousness.

Suddenly, there was a commotion, and I heard the distinct sound of oars pulling hard across the surface of the water. Someone shouted. I heard a strong female voice, and command, in reply, and then I relaxed entirely as I felt new hands on my womb and forehead. I gasped, and my body seemed to lift upward, in a strong, contracted movement. Suddenly, the pain stopped, and I sensed Ilithyia calming.

I reached out with my hand instinctively and touched the woman's face. I tried to open my eyes and part my dry lips, to say thank you.

"Be still now," it was Demeter's voice. "This is a false labor, and I will make it stop. I'm here, Hera, it will be alright."

"But how?" I managed to say, my voice thin.

She leaned down close to my ear, her palm still strong on my head and stomach. "I heard your call, Hera," she said. "Rest now, and we will take you to the Emerald Temple."

When I could be moved Zeus helped carry me to the craft that Demeter and one of her women had arrived in. He beamed at me with every step.

"So, you're a priestess," he said as he laid me in the belly of the boat, wrapping his cloak close about me. "The High Priestess' heir."

His eyes shone with adoration and victory. I didn't mind. I was beyond exhaustion, and it felt good to have him close and to feel his caring. I'd been upset with the way we'd parted, and felt guilty that I hadn't told him about the baby. I kissed him gently as he pressed his lips to mine.

"I'll send you word," I said weakly, as Artemis took her place in front of me and picked up an oar. "It's good to see you, Zeus."

He flashed his cocksure grin, and leaned toward me, whispering in my ear.

"We are meant to be, my love."

Demeter sat at my side and placed her hands on my shoulders.

"We must go," she commanded. She stared at Hades coldly, reaching out a hand to her daughter. Persephone took it, stepped into the craft and sat down by my side. She did not look back at Hades, but her cheeks were wet with tears.

The men pushed the vessel into the water. We were all silent as boat glided into the lake. I took up Persephone's hand and squeezed it weakly, and she placed her arm around me protectively.

"This is a sign, surely," she said to me.

I nodded, though I doubted that either of us knew what it was a sign of. No one could, or would, ignore the apparent hand of destiny in the event of such chance. The High Priestess would now know that the father of my child was leader of the Titan army. Surely Rhea would take every advantage of that and with no resistance from Zeus. Persephone's rendezvous with Hades had also been brought to light, and Demeter, for all her kindness, had a fierce heart. Her devotion to her daughter would not make it easy for Persephone to leave the temple now, or ever.

I leaned back and closed my eyes knowing enough to be afraid of what was going to unfold next.

CHAPTER SIX

I WAS GIVEN A LARGE ROOM in my grandmother's hall where I spent several days recovering. My sister priestesses indulged me with sweet cakes and scented baths and massages with medicinal oils. It was good to be with the women, our chatter and laughter filling the halls of the great house. Medusa was given sanctuary in the temple, and Artemis was welcomed and openly admired, though, to my chagrin, Aphrodite took most of her time. Persephone kept a distance from her mother and the others. Although Demeter was aware of why Persephone had been on that beach, she hadn't brought it to the attention of the other holy mothers. Persephone resumed her duties, but her sadness was apparent in her features.

In the days that followed I tried to keep her close to me. Aphrodite kept Artemis to herself most nights, and so I asked for Persephone to sleep beside me until the baby was again calm in my womb. She was as grateful for the companionship and comfort as I was.

My room was quite large, with its hearth and a tub sunk down into the limestone floor. The windows were broad and arched, bolted closed against the cold nights by wooden blinds intricately carved with spiral designs. The doors to the verandah were the same, the knobs and hinges made of copper, with beautiful stones hammered about the sides. Fresh mint and chamomile wafted from a clay bowl set over a candle on an altar. A bag of birch leaves and pine needles was put by the fire each day, to be thrown over the flames, scenting the room. I had never been so comfortable or well appointed. Persephone shared my delight at our surroundings.

"When I was a child," she told me one night, as we pulled the soft blankets about us and rested our heads on the downy pillows, "I used to sneak up to these apartments when our mothers were called by the High Priestesses and pretended I lived here, that I was queen."

She sighed and reached out for my hand.

"You did not want to be a priestess?" I ventured.

"No."

I rubbed her arm gently.

"Why have you stayed all these years, Persephone?" And then before she could answer, "Why didn't you leave with Hades long ago?"

She wept. I let her spill her tears into the pillow, waiting patiently for her to calm and explain, but I already knew the answer. Love of her mother kept her here, of course, and her loyalty to the temple. These women were her family, and to leave behind this life without her mother's blessing would mean losing everything she'd ever known.

"But why won't Demeter give you her blessing?" I pressed.

"He is a Titan priest," she sniffled. "And his ambitions make my mother wary. She does not trust his love for me, and as I will not be High Priestess when Rhea—" she stopped abruptly, and I could feel the embarrassment rise within her. I wrapped my arm around her reassuringly. She was dear to me. I understood finally what my presence meant in the course of her life, and I felt terrible.

"Now that I'm here, and I have control of the fire element, I'm the High Priestess' heir," I said in a low tone. "I'm sorry, sister."

"No," she insisted, "Please, don't be sorry! I have never wanted to have such responsibility or to be queen in the *Heiros Gamos,* which is what Hades has pressed me for. I am content with temple life, Hera, and I'm so glad you're here." She kissed my forehead. "The truth is, you're saving me from a role I've never wanted."

She lay in my arms, close, with her hand protectively on my belly.

"But now that I'm here, Persephone," I whispered, "you could go with Hades—"

"No," she said resolutely. "I won't ignore the signs. The day on the beach was too clearly a message that I was to return to the temple. What I have with Hades—" She stopped and was quiet for a long moment. "Hades has much to learn, and at times I think I can change him. He does love me, truly, but sometimes love is not enough. I asked the Creator for guidance, and I received it. It wasn't the message I hoped for, but I'm wise enough to follow it."

I nodded my head and sunk down into the pillows. The last candle flame flickered and hissed into the darkness.

"It was a message, wasn't it Persephone?" I whispered. "And we should follow it."

"Yes," she whispered back, squeezing my hand. "It is leading us both somewhere, Hera. I don't know where. I wish I did."

"I do too," I said.

She began to hum a tune I recalled from my months in Athena's house. It was sullen but sweet, and I let it lull me to sleep.

I woke to the sound of Artemis slipping quietly through the door, just as the first light of dawn shone in the hallway outside. She moved to my side of the bed, grinning as I pulled my arms carefully from Persephone's grasp. Artemis eyed me speculatively, but I shook my head and rolled my eyes as I slipped from the bed, pulling on my warm, green mantle. It was irritating that Artemis could not see that she was the only woman I had ever loved or wanted to share my bed with. I knew that she loved me, and was devoted, but she would not come to me as more than a friend. Now that she sensed my connection with Zeus, I feared she would never look at me that way.

Zeus. I struggled with my feelings toward him. There was something there, strong and sure, a warm familiarity and something else I could not name. Perhaps it was the sense of destiny drawing us together to make our child, but I could not be sure. For what drew me to Zeus was nothing like the devoted love I felt for Artemis.

Artemis stood by the door waiting for me to slip on my boots, and I followed her out of the room. I went hurriedly to the privy, while she waited, and then she helped me lumber down the stairs toward the kitchen where I could already smell the porridge and bread wafting through the air.

The cook seemed happy to see me.

"The best medicine is food, and my kitchen has the freshest! I'll fatten you and that baby up yet," she chided, pouring me a steaming bowl and a glass of fresh warm milk. She sent the girl working beside her to the hen house for eggs. Artemis ate with me, ripping the hot bread in two and smearing it with butter and honey. She chatted easily about what she'd seen of the isle and the temple grounds, pointing out that there were deer on the other side and serpents in the caves by the beach. I was surprised to hear this. How had I not known such things even after I'd lived here for almost a full turn of the seasons? She pulled out her knife and sliced another piece of bread, this time handing it to me.

"Aphrodite is being sent to Caledocean," she said at last.

I glanced up at her uneasily. Since my return, Aphrodite had made no secret of her feelings toward me. Although her hair had grown back, lustrous and full, she bore a thin scar on her right cheek that would never go away. I avoided her as much as I could.

"She's asked me to go with her," she finished.

I slid the piece of bread into my mouth and chewed, trying not to react. My eyes rested evenly on the tabletop.

"So, will you go?" I said reaching for the jam.

I could feel Artemis's eyes on me, but I didn't look up to meet her gaze.

"So," she answered slowly, "I wanted to see where you thought you'd be."

I looked up sharply, but the cook was suddenly beside me.

"The eggs are fresh, just what you and the baby need," she said flashing her toothy grin, and handing me a plate.

As I smiled back and reached for the plate, Aphrodite stepped into the room. She sat down on the bench next to Artemis and slid her arms about her waist. Aphrodite leaned forward, whispered something in Artemis's ear and giggled sweetly, kissing her cheek.

My stomach tightened at the sight of it. Nausea threatened to take hold. Pushing the plate away, I pulled myself to my feet. Artemis moved quickly to help me, but I waved her back.

"Hera, please let me help you."

"I don't need your help!" I snapped.

Everyone in the kitchen stood suddenly still and Artemis stepped back.

Before I could say anything, Aphrodite stood up between us and turned to me. Her eyes narrowed and she smiled.

"We understand," she said waving her hand magnanimously. "You are so big with child, you should rest," she said.

"Yes, please excuse me," I murmured, dropping my head and turning toward the door.

Slowly, I made my way back up the stairs to my room. Persephone was awake and helped me ease into the tub, hot water running smoothly through the aqueduct that passed through the iron pipes from the kitchen. I spent the morning this way, meditating in the water, easing my aches and chanting out my loneliness and confusion. I reached deep inside myself to touch Ilithyia, but even she seemed out of reach.

After the mid-day meal, I strolled the gardens for the first time, strong enough to be outside on my own. I stepped into the circle of roses, which my grandmother grew outside her windows, and sat on the stone bench. I intended to let myself drift in their fragrance, but my grandmother appeared at the head of the garden with Demeter and Athena at her side. I struggled to get to my feet before they reached me, but all three waved me down.

"Stay where you are, Hera," my grandmother chided pulling up a wooden chair to sit opposite me.

Demeter and Athena each took a place on either side of me. I shifted uncomfortably by the surprise of their visit. Rhea noticed.

"Don't be alarmed," she said, but her voice was not soothing. "There is a matter we must speak to you about."

Ilithyia stirred. I tightened my grip on my robe, knowing full well the words they would speak. The strange sense of knowing had been with me for months, and now I could plainly see where my destiny was moving me. The dream of the two dragons entwined had returned so many times I couldn't mistake its meaning any longer.

"Zeus," I said, "and the *Heiros Gamos.*"

I could feel the tension ease in both Demeter and Athena, but my grandmother stared at me intently.

"We have had a proposal from his father, Kronos, and it is most intriguing," she said. "And the child, although she will be raised at the temple, does come from Zeus's seed?"

I nodded absently, for everyone knew by now.

"Good," she said. "The flood is coming, Hera, and it will be in your daughter's lifetime. While I wished a different path for you, we cannot ignore the opportunity being presented here."

Demeter reached out and put her warm hand on mine until I relaxed my fists.

"He's offered you a seat on the council, Hera," she said. "It is a tremendous thing, and I'm sure he thinks that you will be easily corralled by Zeus to vote with the Titans, but he has no idea your strength of will and character."

"Or loyalty," Athena added, with a note of pride in her voice.

I smiled at that.

"We have a seat of our own, of course," my grandmother continued, "But to have another vote may make all the difference in the days to come. It is more than we'd hoped for!"

They spoke on of a public union, they would officially call a wedding, and the original Titan palace I would take possession of in the heart of Caledocean. They seemed particularly pleased with this.

"It once belonged to the priestesses of the order of the Rose," Demeter said her voice warm and wistful. "The High Priestess there was a visionary. She spoke of the impending quake and flood that would destroy Atlantis, and of the dragon blood queen that would emerge to lead our people to safety."

Rhea sat back in her chair. She looked older and tired.

"The High Priestess there was known as the Mystical Rose," Rhea said. "She made a holy oil that opened the heart of even the coldest spirit."

"She took the Heiros Gamos with the head of the Titan dynasty to end the first war," Athena went on. She turned to me and took my hand. "You are part of a long line of heroines, those that have given their lives to serve the greater good."

I nodded but did not feel any sense of ease. The burden of the journey before me now rested fully upon my heart. I would not take the Heiros Gamos for love. I would not make my family in the heart of a community of love. Whatever dream I had of living a simple life, with my daughter, at the temple, was gone. I now understood that we would both play a part in a much a bigger plan.

"There is one more thing," my grandmother said, leaning forward in her chair. She spoke slowly as if hesitating.

"When you take the Heiros Gamos you will become the High Priestess of the Emerald Temple as well," my grandmother said.

I stared at her in disbelief.

"But grandmother," I said, emotion rising in my voice, "I'm too young, I'm not ready."

She shook her head and held up a hand.

"Listen to me, it's the only way forward now. You will live in Caledocean and be our voice there and in the council room. And I will stay here and run the temple until your time to return comes. It is what's best, Hera. It is what will best serve our purpose."

I did not respond. I only placed my open palms on my stomach and tried to stay calm.

"You'll be a queen, Hera," Demeter reached out, placing a hand on top of mine. "By taking the rites of the *Heiros Gamos,* you will be Atlantis' queen and Zeus will become king. In this way, a new dynasty will be birthed. And she," Demeter pressed lightly on my hands and belly. "She will be kept safe by this union as well."

I looked up at this last piece. "Safe?" I queried.

The three priestesses nodded in unison. Rhea stood, beckoning me to my feet. Athena and Demeter helped me rise, and the High Priestess moved toward me.

"My granddaughter," she said softly.

She took up my hands in hers and looked up into my face. Her eyes were wise and sad.

"Your daughter will be an heir to the power of the Emerald Temple and an heir to the power of the Titan dynasty. The more power you take, as her mother, the safer she will be."

The reality of her words sunk in, and I breathed heavily. I knew I would do whatever it took to protect this child, my child, *my Ilithyia.*

The loneliness I had been feeling welled up even stronger as I considered how becoming the High Priestess, even in name only, would affect my position with the women around me. Already, I was being treated differently, a curtsey here, or a nod of deference there. The title put a terrible distance between me and my sisters.

"And this… wedding?" I asked.

"It will be soon," Athena said, "while you're still with child. To go to the Heiros Gamos so heavy with child will be a sign of feminine strength and the rebirth of the priestesses' authority."

She was smiling with dignity and pride. All of them were. I thought of Persephone then, and I understood why she'd been unable to turn against them, and leave the temple, even for her own heart's desire.

I forced a smile. I looked at Rhea's expectant face and thought of all the years she'd devoted to saving the feminine face of the divine.

"It shall be as you wish, Grandmother," I said.

That night I turned Persephone away to sit alone on the small couch by the window in my room. I looked out at the moon as I had done so many nights as a child. Sounds of merriment rose from the great hall below. The celebration continued long after my grandmother had announced the Titan proposal to the community, and my acceptance. I had smiled through the event, and let them dance for me, and sing, but when I could, I slipped up the stairs and into the darkness of my room.

The moon glowed down upon me, silent and full of understanding. There was a movement at the door, but I did not turn.

"Hera?" It was Artemis's voice. She didn't wait for me to give her leave, but moved through the room and sat across from me beneath the window. The moon lit up her hair in silver streaks, and for a moment, I imagined what she'd look like old, but then the strange thought came to me that

I would never see her genuinely aged. I touched my head uneasily.

"Do you love him?" she asked.

"I carry his child."

"Yes," her voice was terse, "But do you love him?"

I wasn't sure how to answer. What was love to me? I looked into Artemis's eyes and thought, *I love you.*

"It's for the greatest good," I said. "Hard times are coming to Atlantis, Artemis, and things are going to change. The *Heiros Gamos* is my path."

Abruptly, she leaned forward, very close.

"I can take you from this place," she said, "I can find a way to get you back to your mother, Hera if you don't love him—"

My heart leapt. I felt it beat hard inside my chest. Artemis, my fierce huntress, would not let me go to an empty life. This was her love for me. I could not help myself from reaching out and touching her cheek.

"Thank you," I whispered, "It means everything to me that you... care."

"I do," she said, "Hera, I will not let them use you!"

"No," I said evenly. "It is my choice. I know it is my calling, Artemis. I will marry Zeus at the full moon and begin the life I was destined for."

She sat back in her chair and eyed me for another moment.

I stood up and reached out my hand to her. "Come," I said softly to my friend, "Hold me."

I moved to the bed and slid my heavy body down into the warmth, sighing as I felt Artemis follow, her strong body behind me. Her breasts rested softly against my back as I breathed, and her arm draped protectively about my womb.

I felt Ilithyia reach toward Artemis's open palm, which was splayed across my belly. I comforted myself with the awareness that Artemis unconsciously reached back. For a brief moment, I was held by the love between them, and that was enough.

CHAPTER SEVEN

I ENTERED THE CITY OF CALEDOCEAN in an open-air litter, surrounded by the Emerald Temple warriors. They wore crisp, black linen tunics and carried spears. Emerald sashes bound about their waists denoted my private guard. The banners that waved before and aft held the insignia of the dragon, sewn with vivid green thread. Drummers pounded the way before us.

Athena sat atop her gray at the head of the procession, and a long line of priestesses in their beautiful black robes trailed behind us. My grandmother sat proudly at my side, clothed in her royal green cloak, her fingers and neck decked with gold and jewels.

We entered the walled city by the western gate, passing between two ivory colored towers that spiraled high above us. Wealth was draped over this city, and as we made our way through it, I waved to the crowds instinctively, while my eyes wandered in awe, taking in the grandeur.

The streets were paved and gutted with good gray slabs, and fresh water wells sat every hundred paces. There were many women wearing robes of rare, vivid silks. Even young girls had fine jewels at their throats. The houses that lined the wide streets were well-made of large, pale stones with gutted roofs of red tile. They were well maintained, decorated on the outside with luxurious paints and tiles, each towering above us the height of five men. Most had verandahs crowded with people who looked down on us, cheering and waving emerald scarves as we passed by. Everywhere I looked stood well-dressed and finely groomed folk, waving wildly. Children shook green flags tied on fine willow branches, shouting my name.

I was overwhelmed.

"They honor us!" My grandmother boomed over the din. "There has not been a priestess at the palace in decades."

She pointed to the hills that sprawled in the center of the city where the civic buildings stood. She pointed to the Titan palace, a grand estate sat apart from the rest on one of the lower hills. I reached out unconsciously and gripped her hand. She squeezed it warmly in reassurance.

"Remember, it has a temple of its own, which you will reinstate for the women. It will be open to all factions of the city, those who show us their approval now with this welcoming. You will bring honor and renewal to the Temple of the Rose. Your daughters and their daughters will be priestesses of the Order of the Rose."

She let go of my hand and continued to wave. I compliantly did the same, but my eyes focused on the hill and the round, red building with its gilded dome that stood before it. A thrill ran over my skin.

The procession turned at a street corner and moved down past the hills all the way to the open shore and the large, man-made harbor that wound about itself, in concentric circles. Dozens of ships were docked safely in its folds, and a warren of buildings and workshops spread back toward the city—an impressive sight indeed.

As we climbed through the northern quarter of the city toward the hill and my new home, the houses became even larger and grander. Many were also walled and gated— mini-fortresses within the larger fortress of the city itself, and at its center sat our hill, overlooking all. When we reached the base of the hill, I could see a sprawl of workshops, tanneries and a small marketplace set up about the palace that seemed to form a village of its own.

My body was tired by this time, and my arm was heavy from waving. Even my cheeks ached with the effort of smiling. My grandmother had bidden me wear a simple shift, which exposed my pregnant form, but now I grew cold as the sun dipped lower in the sky. I was relieved when we began the parade up the gently sloped road and through the gates of the Titan palace and the old, priestess temple.

We passed through vast, green gardens and a large stable filled with horses as we made our way to the immense house. Zeus stood at the base of the marble stairway that led to a wide portico held aloft by impressive columns. There were other men gathered about him. I recognized Hades at his right and Ajax a few steps above him, all bedecked in crimson cloaks and bearing the clasp of the house of Titan high on their shoulders. Beside Zeus stood a very tall man, with a fine face and brooding eyebrows that were too straight. I took him to be Zeus's father, the patriarch, Kronos. He had a hard, cold look, his white beard stark against his skin, but he had a power about him that I could feel even from a distance. I thought him to be more clever, like Hades than strong, like Zeus, who stood bare-chested in the ceremonial waistband of twisted leather wound about a short skirt of gold. He looked at me warmly, his wide shoulders and tightly muscled limbs gleaming from the oils they'd rubbed into his body.

I relaxed when I saw him move toward me, hands out-stretched. The anxiety that had lived in me through the last weeks of preparation eased, and I reassured myself that I was doing the right thing. For, although I had consigned myself to the *Heiros Gamos* as my destiny, there was something that unnerved me about these circumstances, something unwavering that pressed upon my inner senses—something was out of place.

I pushed it away from me as they set our litter down at Zeus's feet. He helped me to the ground. Kronos reached for my grandmother's hand. Together, we strode up the steps and into the palace.

Zeus put his arm about my shoulders covetously, showing me from room to room.

My body tingled with delight as Zeus held me, showing off the grandeur of my new surroundings. I hadn't realized that I'd missed him until he took my hand. I felt stronger in his presence and much reassured. Zeus was nearly glowing. His charm was at the surface as he guided me to the hall where we would receive our guests. I stopped at the door in amazement: it even rivaled the hall of the Emerald Temple. One wall was completely open to the magnificent vista of the city and the sea. I hadn't realized how high up we must have traveled in our procession.

A long white table was laid out in the middle of the room and covered from one end to the other with delectable foods. Our large party filled the room and Kronos directed us to take our places at the feasting table. Dozens of new faces pressed in upon us, and I was introduced to a throng of dignitaries and leaders. Music played somewhere in the corners of the hall, and we ate and drank and talked late into the evening.

My grandmother guided me expertly through the introductions, alerting me with subtle gestures when a person was of importance to our plans, or if they were to be avoided. I smiled cordially and with what grace I could muster, as the exhaustion of the day swept over me.

My grandmother was pleased.

I felt Zeus watching me from time to time; when I looked his way, he met my gaze with a look of satisfaction and regard. I couldn't help but notice that most of the people thronging him were female, including my sister priestesses. At one point I spied Aphrodite leaning on his arm, and a cold tension moved through me until Artemis joined her, and she let Zeus go. She slid her arm about Artemis's waist before she looked out across the crowd and smiled coldly as she caught my eye.

When the sun finally set, I caught Athena's attention. She gathered my guard about me, and I bowed to my guests and let her take me to my room. It was lavishly laid out with a courtyard and garden of its own. There was a small stone alcove with an altar on one side. There I let Medusa free from her hiding place about my waist.

"This entire wing shall be run by you, Hera," Athena said, pointing to the many rooms that surrounded my own. "There are priestesses just down the hall, and they will come to bathe and dress you." She raised her hand as I protested. "No, you must accept this as the requirement of your station. This is what people will expect, and you must gain their respect by adhering to their customs."

I sat down on a padded couch by the crackling fire and put my hands to my head, wearily. She sat down beside me.

"I know this is…different," she continued more gently. "A far cry from the freedom of your childhood, but you'll grow accustomed to it. Enjoy what you can, Hera, for with this wealth comes a responsibility that few could bear. Tomorrow, you shall become a queen."

I sighed, rubbing my temples in small circles. The baby kicked, and the fire crackled. Something felt wrong, but I couldn't determine what it was.

Athena called in a young priestess who helped me out of the light tunic and into a warm nightgown. She turned back the thick blankets of my bed and let down thin netting that draped the frame.

"There is a bell here by the bed," she said, "I sleep lightly and will come anytime you call."

As she bowed her head in deference, my throat tightened, and I held back tears. *Servants,* I thought, sadly. *They are not my friends.* There would always be a distance between us, a hierarchy that couldn't be breached. I lay awake in the bed, wishing for Artemis. If she'd come to me this night and offered me escape, I was keenly aware that I might accept it.

The fire hissed again as the flames turned into glowing coals, and the warmth seemed to seep out of the room. I rolled myself awkwardly onto my side. My belly was inconveniently large now; the skin pulled tight across me like the shell of an egg. It wouldn't be long before Ilithyia would be in my arms, a few weeks at most. I tried to let the thought of her pacify me, but still, I trembled beneath my blankets.

I shut my eyes and slept restlessly until finally, the soft tide of a dream swept me away in it.

Mist. The sea. I shook my head in the dream as if I could wake myself from it, but instead, I only saw more vividly. I looked about me, and the place seemed familiar. It was the prow of a ship.

"Lady," a man's deep voice came out of the gray before me.

His form was ethereal, but I could make out dark hair curling to his bare shoulders, the ceremonial waistcloth with its golden skirt hanging from thin hips. Was this Zeus? I reached out, but his form and face shimmered and receded further. Why could I not make him out?

"I've dreamt of you all my life," he said reaching toward me, but now his form was only a thin line of light. "Trust your instincts, trust in me…"

"Zeus?" I cried out uncertainly and then in desperation. "Zeus!"

My eyes flew open. The room was dimly lit now with a soft orange glow. I pulled the pillows about me and wept.

CHAPTER EIGHT

MY PARENTS ARRIVED EARLY THE NEXT MORNING, and Mother came with the women of the temple to prepare me for the ceremony of the *Heiros Gamos,* the sacred union. I was relieved to see her. The anxiety that moved over my body was quieted in her presence.

"Mother!"

She took me in her arms for only a moment then pushed me away gently. Her eyes rested on my belly.

"You look beautiful, Hera," she said. "I've missed you!"

We both began to cry, and she took me in her arms again for a long time. When we pulled away, Demeter stepped up to Mother's side and kissed her cheek.

"It's gone by so fast hasn't it?" she said. "I remember when we were each with child."

Mother shook her head, and they laughed. It was the first time I'd seen Mother at ease and even laughing in front of the women she'd once been so close to. Others approached her with congratulations, and for the first time, I understood how my choice would affect Mother. She would regain some stature at the Emerald Temple and in the eyes of the people; my reign would forever reflect upon her. I felt this as another responsibility added to all the others, and again, I felt ill.

The women discarded their ceremonial robes to place me in a large pool filled with seawater, warmed from the copper pipes that ran beneath it. They ceremonially washed me to let the salt water purify my body and mind, easing my emotions so that I could come to rest in the river of consciousness that made up my very being. My grandmother stripped herself of her clothes and she and Athena, and Demeter floated me in the liquid womb, hands beneath my back and neck so that I shut my eyes and collapsed into the vast spaciousness before birth and after death, the immortal perspective in which all my fear and mistrust fell away. There was peace here, and contentment within. Whatever lay ahead, I knew that this place existed within me, and knowing this strengthened me to do what was before me now.

When I was serene, they placed me in a tub of fresh, warm water and scrubbed my skin until it was pink. They chanted as they worked over me. I listened contentedly to the soft swish of the water as the women dunked their sponges and then squeezed them above my shoulders and head. From beyond the window, I could see the bright, blue sky and feel the breeze that blew in off the sea. From far below us on the hill, I could already hear the sounds of hammer and horses as the dioceses and feasting tents were erected. Laughter floated on the wind.

They lifted me from the tub, and dried and rubbed me with sacred oils. Geranium was massaged into my hair and scalp, and chamomile into my belly to keep Ilithyia calm through the ceremony. The room filled with fragrance as they burned the frankincense and myrrh. They pleated my hair in long, waving strands and bound these with ribbons and pearls. My dress was brilliant red, the color of woman's blood, to symbolize my power and fertility, with a darker, crimson robe laid about my shoulders. They tied a girdle about my waist to accentuate my ripe form and strung winter flowers about my neck. Medusa slid beneath the garment, warm across my belly, out of sight.

Mother directed them as they lined my eyes with black kohl, and painted my feet and hands with the intricate serpent designs of my lineage. I hummed and chanted with my sister priestesses as they worked.

The drum stopped beating.

We all stood in silence as they pulled forth a long, polished copper mirror, and I beheld a reflection of my form shimmering on its surface. My face was full now with my pregnancy but in a most pleasing way. My breasts, which lay slightly exposed above my girdle, were heavy and round, and my skin was darker than it had been before, which pleased me. Rhea laid the emerald medallion, symbol of the High Priestess of the Emerald Temple and her house, about my neck. It glistened in the light of the noonday sun that shone strongly through the window.

She broke the silence, then, ushering us into a processional line, signaling Mother to come to the front.

"You will lead her to the altar, Sophia," she said.

Mother stared at her in surprise. Rhea half scowled at Mother, waving her forward.

"It is tradition," Rhea stated, "you *are* Hera's mother!"

She stepped toward Mother and pulled another necklace from her robe. It had a smaller emerald set between the two copper dragon figures, as did mine. Her hands shook slightly as she held it up to show Mother the stone in the light.

"It is part of your heritage, Sophia," she continued. "You would honor us all by wearing it."

A heavy silence hung in the room as Mother shifted uncomfortably. The old pain between them had softened, but it was not gone.

I glanced at Demeter for a sign, but she only stood quietly at Mother's side. Their timeless friendship was palpable.

"But I am no longer a priestess of the temple," Mother said.

"You are my daughter," Rhea countered. "And this is mine to give."

Rhea stepped forward and placed the medallion about Mother's neck. Rhea's eyes softened as she stepped back and beheld the sight.

"My daughter and granddaughter," she said quietly. "I had hoped to live long enough to see such a day."

Mother placed her hand on the jewel and smiled.

There was a loud sound as the big doors were thrown open and Athena appeared with her armor in place, sword at her side. The thick bronze bands, signifying her leadership, wound about her upper arms and calves. Power shone in her eyes. I expected her to direct us to the hall that led outside to the ceremonial grounds where I could now hear people gathering in masses, but instead she signaled Rhea and me to follow. We stepped into the corridor where her soldiers stood in fine armor and gripped their spears straight. We turned the other way and headed toward one of the small side chambers.

"The high priest of the Titans waits for us with Hades and Kronos," she said.

I could feel Rhea brace herself before we stepped inside, and I put my hand over my womb instinctively.

There were elaborate greetings, and Kronos swept forward, took my hand in his and kissed it. Hades didn't move but eyed me. The high priest of the Temple of Light, the Lucifer, stood by his side with a similar look. I felt his eyes rest for a long moment on the emerald medallion at my throat. He shook his head so slightly that it could easily have been missed. He was a short man, and slight of feature, but his eyes were intense, and he carried his head high. I was surprised to see him garbed in a robe of black, the color of night and the feminine force. Hades was dressed the same.

The priest stepped toward my grandmother with a short, natural stride as if they were old friends. To my shock, he addressed her by name. Rhea's body tensed as he did so and I moved forward, throwing off Kronos's hand, a surge of animosity moving over me. My grandmother held up her hand and stopped me at her side. I sensed the ground beneath her rising into her strong limbs, and an invisible shield seemed to envelop us.

"Why have you called us here, Lucifer?" Rhea asked.

The man waved elaborately at me, and my gown. "We sent her an appropriate dress," he said, waving at the girl in the corner of the room which held a white linen garment, embroidered with glistening beads.

I recognized the insignia sewed about the hem as Zeus's lightning bolt. White was the traditional color of the Titan banner.

"I'm not a Titan, yet," I snapped.

My grandmother smiled. "What Hera means," she said smoothly, "is that people would not understand the symbolism intended if a High Priestess were to wear a garment of white. Red is the ceremonial color of the High Priestess, while white—" she almost spat the word and did not finish.

"But the dress we sent—"

Rhea turned away from the priest as if he weren't there and looked at Kronos. "Surely you didn't intend my grand-daughter to stand in ceremony without her robes of power to adorn her?"

Hades grimaced, and the Lucifer's face turned red, but neither spoke as she addressed Kronos. I took careful note of my grandmother's trick. The older man faltered beneath Rhea's intense stare.

"Of course not, my apologies," Kronos said smoothly. "There must have been some mistake."

The high priest shuffled his feet as if to interrupt, but Hades laid a heavy hand on his shoulder, and the man stilled. When Kronos bowed to Rhea, Hades stepped forward and pointed to the door.

"Come, Father," he said, "we should take our places and let the Lucifer begin the ceremony. The crowd is large, and they grow restless."

He brushed up against me as he passed toward the door with Kronos's at his side, which I knew not to be an accident. This vexed me, but I hadn't time to react as my grandmother ushered me to Athena's guard.

Athena leaned close to my ear and spoke beneath her breath, "The Lucifer is the most powerful of all the priests," she said. "Be wary, Hera."

Then I was swept up in my retinue's long procession down the hall and toward the crowd and assembly of priests and priestesses that waited at the altar. Mother walked beside me until we reached the stairs then she squeezed my shoulders and kissed my cheek, and took her place before me in the procession.

When we emerged from the palace, onto the verandah, I gasped: the vast field before us was thronged with people.

Scented smoke rose from small fires laid with linden and sagebrush set beside our path. A euphony of harmonics lifted my spirits as I walked. The singers stood beside and before us, and even aloft on the balconies that looked out over the scene. They sang the serpents' song, the words a winding of the male and female in one body, as one being. I swayed with the tune, the strong male voices grounding me to the earth and the high, light tones of the women opening my mind to the sky above.

Hands reached out to touch me as I passed, but Athena's guard kept them at bay. The altar was set upon a high stage with a shell-shaped stone behind it that seemed to amplify the voices of the singers.

Rhea was on the diocese next to Lucifer who stood stiffly and with great pomp. A red scarf was now laid across his shoulders. I looked at the group of priests that stood behind him noting that they were dressed the same. I steadied myself. Why were the men wearing our colors? My grandmother's words about the priests and their desire to grab power passed through my mind. I tried to tell myself that Zeus had no part in this, but as I neared the stairs to the altar, he stepped out to take my hand and I faltered. He was garbed in a long white robe as was expected, but his cape was the same color as my own.

Zeus helped me up the stairs, and we took our places before the assembly. I'd never seen so many people at once, and I searched the faces, relieved to see my father's steady gaze. I could see the love in his eyes. I tried to relax my mind in the strength of his gaze, for there was indeed no going back now.

We turned our backs to the witnesses and knelt before my grandmother who anointed our heads and blessed us. Then the Lucifer and Hades approached. I shivered as Hades made the sign of peace above my head and marked my brow with ash. When the priest took up his staff and bade us repeat our vows, Medusa, who'd been coiled warm against my waist, rearranged herself beneath my robe. I tried to concentrate on the priest's words as she wound her way up my back and over my shoulders, but the words seemed different than the ones that had been approved, and completely out of order. He spoke of the power of the Titan dynasty and the rule of kings rather than unity and love.

The Lucifer took a step away from us and turned to the crowd.

"The time has come," the Lucifer said in an enigmatic voice, holding up his hands directing everyone to listen. "Long have we waited for a leader to rise amongst us, one who could lead our armies in our efforts to expand Atlantis' frontiers. Long have we searched for a man who could wield the sword of Atlantis' power and prepare the way for our people's new lives. Now, we've found that man, the hand that will carry our sword." He turned slightly toward us as he spoke this last and his left hand gestured to Zeus. "The priesthood of Atlantis has agreed with the council that Zeus, son of Kronos and heir to the third kingdom of the Titan dynasty, shall be Atlantis' sacred king!"

Cheers rose from the crowd. Soldiers along the far gates waved their unsheathed swords. I looked at Zeus quizzically, not sure what was going on, and he glanced back at me, just as surprised. Perspiration had broken out across his forehead, and his mouth was grim.

The Lucifer held up his hands once again, a big smile on his face.

"The priests of Atlantis have watched over our people for many generations, providing healers and warriors, sanctuaries and teachers. We've given you schools and built places to worship the great creator, the father by whose seed we are formed."

At this, I heard my grandmother shift on the platform behind us. I sensed her agitation and the strong willfulness it took to hold herself in check. I could see Athena's hand resting tight on her sword hilt and the horror in the faces of my sister priestesses who looked on from their seats beside the altar. Even Zeus shook his head, but there were hundreds here, witnessing, and I could sense his conflict. He wasn't the sort of man to risk making a fool of himself in front of so many onlookers.

The Lucifer wasn't finished. He seemed to grow in stature with the cheering of the crowd, a breeze-catching up his cape in a dramatic effect. Again, he held up his hands for attention.

"The Father has guided the priesthood of Atlantis to support our kings in the service of their dynasties, service that has led to the wealth and supremacy of Atlanteans in the world beyond our borders." The priests, who I now realized were strategically clustered in groups throughout the crowd, applauded loudly as if on cue. While they cheered and pounded their hands together, others joined in with them, but I could see that not all in the crowd were moved. People's faces had dropped, and women were looking at one another expectantly.

"Yes, yes!" the Lucifer cried out encouraging the clamor. Then as things died down, "This marriage is a symbol of Atlantean power and the new order of things. This *Heiros Gamos* will be a model for future generations, as Atlanteans reach beyond our borders and bring a better way of life to the people of the tribes!"

Meanwhile, Medusa moved over my skin, sending shudders down my spine. With my inner voice, I willed her to be still, but she paid me no heed, draped herself over my shoulder beneath my cloak and headed toward my arm. I shuddered. Zeus looked at me, worriedly, but I tried to allay his fear with a smile.

As the priest pulled out the leather cord with which he would symbolically bind our wrists, he grasped my hand in his steel grip and thrust it into Zeus's. His voice was loud and stern. "With this cord, I bind Hera to Zeus, woman to man, priestess to priest."

I gasped and tried to pull back my hand, but the Lucifer held me fast, draping the cord over my wrist until suddenly, Medusa's head sliced out from beneath the cuff of my gown, her fangs bared, hissing.

Zeus pulled back, but I gripped his hand tight, and he froze. Medusa rose up and splayed her hood out wide. I heard shouts from the witnesses and women's screams, and then my grandmother's loud laughter.

The priest veered back at the sight of the snake, let go of my hand and dropped the cord on the ground. Hades stumbled back behind him, his eyes wide and furious. He pulled the short blade off the altar and raised it above his head to strike. I tried desperately to control the anger that rose up inside of me now, knowing that with my child so close to her time I couldn't dare use the fire to defend us.

Zeus collected himself, squeezing my hand slightly in reassurance.

Medusa wound her body about both our wrists.

I felt my father moving from his place below the altar and heard Artemis's silent voice calling Medusa down, but the snake continued to rear her head.

My grandmother, the true High Priestess of the Emerald Temple, moved into action. She rushed in front of Hades shoving him hard to the side, holding up her hands.

"The Draconigena!" Her deep, magnetic voice thundered up from her belly for all to hear. "The dragon has returned to bind this sacred marriage!"

The people shouted, and I heard the words taken up, repeated again and again: "Draconigena, Draconigena!"

The priest's face had gone red as Athena reached his side with two of her warriors holding him firmly in place. Kronos's face was pale as he reached for Hades's wrist and pulled him back to his feet. Kronos took the sacred blade from Hade's shaking hand and put it back on the altar with as much dignity as he could muster.

Rhea held up her hands for silence and moved before Zeus and me, reaching down fearlessly toward Medusa, and lifting our hands so all could see.

"The truth of the *Heiros Gamos* has always been and will always be that we are all bound to each other, male and female faces of the One!" she called out as the crowd quieted. "There is no escaping the reality of the dragon! *We are all immortal!* Blessed Be!"

The drumbeat again in the distance. People clapped, and stomped, shouting and singing.

Rhea slid her arm beneath my own and helped Zeus pull me to my feet. Medusa dropped her hood and stopped hissing at my grandmother's approach, and settled down about my wrist. Zeus and I turned toward the ecstatic crowd and lifted our hands, bound by the snake, as they cried out again and again, "Draconigena!"

My grandmother let them gain momentum, which raised a cone of power about us all. I swayed beneath the weight of it, and my arm grew weak. I reached out with my mind and summoned Medusa back beneath my gown. This time she heeded my call. Zeus moved closer to me as we lowered our hands and let me lean against him. The baby wrestled within me, and I could feel the heat of tears and exhaustion moving over my cheeks. I gripped Zeus's arm tightly.

Rhea repositioned herself at our sides as she raised her voice one last time.

"Hera and Zeus, we bind you in the sacred marriage for now and always. May love keep you and bless you with the knowledge of itself all the days of your lives, and through all the lives you will ever live! May you come to know the truth and stand as the immortals you are. Beyond birth and death may you come to know that you are creation and creator, formlessness and form!" She laid her palm on top of ours and bound us beneath her grasp. "Blessed Be."

As Zeus and I joined the crowd in sealing the prayer, the power swept over us joining my fate to Zeus's forever.

"Blessed be," I said.

CHAPTER NINE

I LEANED HARD ON ZEUS as I made my way toward the stairs to leave the diocese. We passed by the chairs where we were supposed to receive our guests and give our blessings. I gestured to Athena for a quick retreat. She was at my side at once, her shield on her arm, pressing through the crowd and guiding us back to my room. Her women moved in a long line on either side of us as we made our way slowly through the crowd. People pushed at us from all sides, begging our blessings and we reached out to them on our way, as best we could, but the pressure of the day and the alarming behavior of the Lucifer had forced us from our course. Rhea waved graciously, but she too urged Athena forward. At some point, Mother was at my side, and Artemis was behind me. As we reached the stairs, I was near to collapse, and Zeus slid his arm about my waist, half carrying me to my room. A rolling wave of applause washed over us as we moved out of sight of the crowd, and I struggled to keep my composure. The moment we were down the hall and inside my room with the door closed, my legs buckled. I shut my eyes and grabbed my abdomen where a pain stabbed hard. Hands moved all about me, lifting, and I heard myself moan.

The baby.

"Zeus," I whimpered in a voice full of pain.

He grasped me close, and his voice came warm and soft. "I'm right here," he said. "The baby will be alright, and you're in the best hands."

Demeter moved close and placed her palms on my sacrum and then signaled them to move me to the couch. She said words that soothed me, and the wave of pain released me. I breathed deep and nodded. Yes, the moment was passing, all would be well. I opened my eyes and looked about the room. A thick tension hung about us. Mother came and sat beside me. Artemis took my other side. I gave Medusa over to Artemis's arm. Zeus still kneeled before me, holding my hand. He looked at me with his cool blue eyes and said, "I love you, Hera."

My mother laid a light hand on my shoulder and reached out the other to Zeus. "You're a good man, Zeus," she said.

Athena made a hard, sarcastic sound as she put down her shield and turned to Zeus. He stood as she took a strong step toward him.

"A good man?" she snapped. "Your priest—" she began, waving her hand harshly, but Rhea stepped between them.

"It was not my doing," Zeus declared. "The position of Lucifer is a powerful one, but I swear to you I'll see justice done. I'll have him removed!"

There was a tone of devotion in Zeus's voice. I knew he was trying to champion me, and my people, yet his zeal made me uncomfortable. I knew him too well. He would make this thing right to improve my image of him, but I wished he would do it on principle. But he was not that kind of man, and I knew this was one of the many things I was going to have to accept.

Tears came now to my eyes, but they were soft and quiet, and shed only for myself.

A loud clanking of arms came from outside the door. Athena drew her sword and was outside in a moment. I heard raised voices, and then Zeus moved toward the door, which he flung open, exposing Kronos and Hades on the other side. Hades signaled his men to stand down, and the line of warriors put up their swords.

"I've only brought them for the couple's protection," he declared, face to face with Athena who still gripped tight to the handle of her blade.

"After today's display by the Titan dynasty, I will post temple guards that I can trust to protect my queen," Athena snapped.

Rhea's face was grim, but she snapped a command, and Athena stood down, letting Kronos and Hades pass into the room, their guard surrounded by temple warriors bearing spears. Artemis slipped her hand into mine as Kronos, his look apologetic, swept toward me and kneeled down shaking his head. His dark eyes looked sincere as he spoke, but everything in my body shied away from him.

"My deepest apologies," he said. "The Lucifer was acting on his own and didn't speak for the house of Titan."

He stood then and turned to my grandmother. "He has been removed and will be tried. I will personally bring charges against him."

Rhea forced a smile and nodded. "And who will be named in his place, Kronos? Who shall become the new Lucifer of the House of Titan?"

Hades stepped forward magnanimously. "I have already been named," he said.

Demeter took a startled step back, shaking her head, but my grandmother stood still and held his gaze. Her high cheekbones burned with color, but she spoke evenly.

"The Emerald Temple welcomes you then, Lucifer. We shall look forward to seeing how you use your vote at the council."

The corners of Hades's lips moved slightly and then he turned away from her abruptly.

"A big day for us all," Hades said into the stunned silence of the room. "The people shall have a new generation of leaders."

My breath became shallow as he spoke and a wave of nausea moved over me so that his voice faded and I swallowed hard. I knew I should stand and say something, to show myself a part of this hierarchy and to defend the temple, but instead, I felt that I would swoon. Artemis squeezed my hand, and someone called Demeter's name. A warm gush of water moved down between my legs and spilled onto the floor.

"No," I said opening my eyes again and clutching my stomach. "It's still too soon!"

The men stared at me blankly, but Athena moved quickly toward them, backing them to the door. Demeter laid her hand on my abdomen as it had another spasm.

"The baby is coming," she said, her voice low. "Stay calm, Hera; she is early, but it's not too soon."

Zeus moved toward me, but I shook my head, clutching tight to Artemis's hand.

"Leave this to the women, Zeus," Mother said, moving to his side and leading him toward the door. "When Hera wants you there, we will call."

Zeus stopped at the door a pained look on his face.

"I'll be right here, Hera," he said his voice strong with devotion. "Forever."

I looked up into his eyes, and something old passed between us. Was it a memory? Was it love? I could not say, but there was a bond here I would never be able to deny.

"I'll be alright," I said, gripping tighter to Artemis's hand. "Go now, Zeus. Go."

Hades put his hand on his brother's arm, and Zeus nodded. The men followed him out of the room.

There was a bustling movement all about me, and in the whirl, most of the women left the room except for Artemis and Mother, who were on either side of me, and Demeter, whose hands pressed firmly against my back. They helped me out of my gown and into a loose robe, and then we moved down the hall to the women's bathhouse.

The day had been long now, and everyone's nerves were frayed, but the women gathered around me and spoke encouraging words. They made me eat sweet bread and honey and drink a strong tea. Mother and Artemis walked me back and forth across the floor as the labor pains bore down upon me.

Outside the high-pitched trumpets blew a celebratory tone and I knew the word had gone out that I was in labor. To our people, this would be seen as the greatest of blessings, a sign of new beginnings and the fertility of the sacred union. Within the room, I struggled not to blame the event itself for bringing my daughter too early into the world.

Artemis seemed to know what I was thinking, and she stopped my pacing, turning me to face her. A look of excitement and wonder shone in her eyes. "It's a strong sign," she said firmly. "The birth of your heir on the eve of the *Heiros Gamos!* There's nothing at all to worry about."

She leaned toward me then, suddenly, taking my face in both of her hands and kissed me full on the mouth. I shuddered with delight, and my whole body relaxed into her.

"Soon, we'll have her in our arms!" she said.

I smiled for the first time.

Mother moved back to my side, and together they guided me into the water just as the pain wrapped itself about me. I labored in the pool, Demeter and the warm water easing the pain. A fire blazed warmly in the hearth, throwing off enough heat that we could keep open the shutters on the arched windows that looked out onto the courtyard beyond. The sounds of the festivities floated in on a light breeze, and I could see by the dim yellow rays cast against the far wall that the sun had almost set.

I eased back into the water, letting the women float me there as I willed my daughter to position herself correctly inside my womb. My eyes rested on the paintings emblazoned on the walls of the circular chamber. They were painted with a deep burgundy, like a woman's blood, and thick white strokes of sacred symbols were inscribed upon it. The life-sized figure of the cow, full-bellied and pregnant, was the first sight to greet me. There were snakes painted in a coiled position, entwined together, shedding their skins. Before me branched out the sacred tree, symbol of fertility and immortality. I stared at the tree intensely as the next spasm came and then the next, meditating on its bridge-like quality uniting the world above with the world below, and I opened myself to do the same. I became this sacred tree as I labored, the bridge between the invisible and visible worlds. I held onto this thought as the pains swept over me and I surrendered myself to them.

Outside the birthing room, in the outer chamber, I heard women, priestesses from our temple, beginning the birth chant, which they would sing in turns until the baby was born. The sounds they made were low and rhythmic and gave me strength. In a short time, I heard it picked up by voices outside the window as well. Mother went to the open arch and looked out.

"They come from the festival, Hera," she said, surprise in her tone. "There is a long line still filing in. Some are dressed in finery, and others are common folk, but they are all women."

"It has been a very long time since women have gathered here," Demeter said with joy and pride. "The feminine revival has already begun."

The singing continued in long, low tones. Their voices floated up to me like clouds in the wind. I opened myself to the sound so that my daughter might hear them calling to her, welcoming her home.

As the twilight came and passed, the rushes were lit in the room and more wood placed on the fire. I alternately paced and floated, and sweet oils were massaged into my back and feet. Persephone came to relieve our mothers, bringing food and drink, but Artemis would not leave my side.

Many hours later I was drained beyond anything I'd ever known, and sunk down into the water wearily, moaning. A pain so great I could hardly breathe seized me. I wanted to give up, to become hysterical with exhaustion and pain, but instead, I chanted and panted through the waves while the women continued to sit the vigil, singing for me, and my daughter.

When finally the midwife pressed her hand between my legs and felt for the baby's head, I leaned back in the water, Artemis's strong form behind me.

"I must push!" I said.

The midwife shook her head. "Wait, Hera! Breathe like a panting pup; it will help you to hold back!" But the urge bore down on me. My body rocked, and the pain came again, so that I thought I'd split open, but still the midwife bade me wait. I cried out with frustration, shaking my head desperately and thrashed about the water, even as Mother begged me to be still. When I opened my eyes I saw for the first time, a real panic in Mother's face and tears stood in her eyes.

"The babe must be turned," she tried to explain, but her voice caught in her throat, and I sensed her anxiety. She feared for both the child and me. Suddenly, my grandmother stood at the edge of the steps to the pool, her magnificent round form a pillar of strength. I said something to her, half hysterical, and I couldn't make out my own words as I lifted outside my body from the overwhelming sensations.

"Don't push!" cried the midwife again as she slid her hand between my outstretched legs.

"I have to," I pleaded, arching in agony.

Mother gripped tight to my hand and urged me to gain control. I heard the desperate warning in her voice and tried to reign in my panicked mind. My grandmother stepped into the pool with her robes on, sending a warm wave of water up over my bare breasts.

"Open your eyes, Hera," she commanded, her voice pressing me back down into my form. "Open your eyes, child, and look at your mother."

My eyes flew open. I stared into Mother's wide eyes, and the pain eased a little.

"It was the same with me," my grandmother said, taking up my other hand in hers. "Sophia came too soon and feet first, but look what perfection she is."

Mother turned toward my grandmother with her eyes full of tears.

"Both of you must rest now in the competent care of these women's hands, and the strength of your love for each other. You will not say goodbye to each other this night."

Mother nodded vigorously and pushed back the hair from my face and kissed my cheek. Another wave came, and then another on top of it, but I eased my mind deep into Mother's love, and the kindness and caring all about me. I willed myself to wait, legs shaking. More women entered the pool and pressed their soft bodies against me to still my trembling limbs.

One more sharp pain and then the midwife bade me push at last, and I bore down into a terrible, necessary burning. And then the pressure released from me, the baby gliding like a fish into my grandmother's open hands. I saw her body shimmering in the water as the women moved quickly to unbind her cord and float her to the surface. I was hardly aware of the tears that rolled down my cheeks or the glistening wet of my grandmother's eyes as she laid a small blanket over my breast and handed Ilithyia to me. I held her small, perfect form in my two hands and laid her upon my chest. The long cord that ran from her belly still joined us as I pressed her gently to my breast. Artemis still cradled us both in the warm water, and it lapped onto Ilithyia's tiny feet.

I relaxed back into Artemis's arms as the baby clenched my breast and latched onto my nipple with her ruby lips and suckled. There were sighs of delight from all around the room, and hushed words of congratulations and blessing. Mother was crying deeply now, touching the baby's cheek gently with her hand. My grandmother was still in the water beside her. I looked at them both.

"We are four generations," I said through my tears.

"Priestesses born," Mother added in a soft voice.

My grandmother laid a hand on Mother's shoulder. "Priestesses still," she said.

Mother's lips were quivering, but she didn't speak. My grandmother drew her into a deep embrace.

"If I have to say it a thousand times before you will believe me, I will, Sophia," she said cradling her daughter. "I was wrong, and I'm sorry for it. I love you."

We stayed in the pool for a long while, Artemis taking Ilithyia as I passed the afterbirth. Mother clamped and cut the cord, and Demeter took it with the afterbirth and placed them in earth to be buried on the morrow beneath a tree. Women helped me from the tub, and dried and dressed me in a warm gown and then I took my daughter in my arms, wrapped in warm, soft wool, and walked to the wide window where the women still gathered chanting beneath the moon. The moonlight illuminated the child in my arms as I appeared, and slowly, the women stopped singing. The silence filled me again with emotion as we stared at one another beneath the silver glow from the sky.

We are one; I thought as I held my babe to my heart, and bowed to them.

I was taken to my bed, and there I fell into a deep sleep. Artemis woke me gently when it was time to feed Ilithyia. "Zeus came and consecrated her with ash," she whispered.

I grimaced. I hadn't had the strength to show her to him myself, and I was glad the women had brought him in. I shut my eyes and slept again.

It was not until noon of the next day that I awoke. Ilithyia lay quiet in the crook of my arm. Artemis lay on the other side of her, still sleeping.

A thrill ran through me. Ilithyia's eyes were open, staring as if at me, though I knew she could not see me yet, the thin line of her mouth opening over her tiny fist. I uncovered her body to count each finger and toe. I breathed in her fresh scent and stretched out my hand across her small frame so that she would know my touch. Her skin was soft and white; her head already had a shocking black mass of hair like her fathers. She shut her tiny eyes as I wrapped her tight, swaddling her. Then I brushed my lips gently against the soft, dark hair on her head, which had been anointed with lavender and rose.

Artemis was staring at me when I looked up, her large, dark eyes glistening. She reached out and placed her hand over mine on Ilithyia's small form.

"She's beautiful," I whispered.

"You're beautiful, Hera," she whispered back.

CHAPTER TEN

THE DAYS PASSED SLOWLY. Winter had taken hold, and the fires were lit in our rooms even during the day. My parents returned to the village, but Artemis stayed on, her bond with Ilithyia evident. Zeus came and went, enjoying his daughter, but far from infatuated with her. As I kept him from my bed while I nursed her, he seemed content to enjoy his new role as a king.

When Ilithyia had passed nine full moons, and the midwife assured my grandmother she would live, word was sent across the land of Atlantis that the Draconigena had an heir. My grandmother confirmed her as my successor, and gifts were sent from the great houses throughout Caledocean along with tedious visits from their leaders. The household settled into a routine of entertaining, and I was forced quickly into my new roles as queen and High Priestess.

I was now surrounded by elaborate finery, adorned with jewels and silken gowns. I attended to routine tasks, political obligations and the restoration of the temple, which showed its years of neglect. My education in the mystical arts came to a halt as I turned all my attention to these worldly matters while trying to spend precious time with my daughter.

The mornings were my best opportunity to be with Ilithyia. She and Artemis would play on the floor about me while my attendants tended to the laborious ritual of making up my person each day. Several women pinched rouge on my cheeks and pressed berries to my lips. Henna was painted in elaborate patterns about my feet and hands, and gowns were made to shape my body, which had grown quite thin while Ilithyia fed. And my hair! They would make it up in splendid curls when we dined with dignitaries, or soft ringlets when I led services in the temple. They'd pull it high atop my head with ornate decorations on days I went out riding.

Artemis often sat in the room playing with Ilithyia watching my agonizing rite of formality. I envied her comfortable tunic and leggings, her hair down her back in a simple braid. Ilithyia, however, seemed to take great pleasure in the pains I was going through.

On the morning of my first council, she was at my feet, crawling through the gowns I'd tossed on the floor, and delighting in the combs and pins I splayed out before her despite my attendants' protests. After far too much pampering of my face, I waved my women away and got down on the rug with Ilithyia and Artemis, letting my daughter play with the dangles in my ears and the gold and copper circles that hung at my wrists, all of which she placed in her mouth before handing them back to me, covered in drool. I laughed out loud.

"Lady, you will be late," the older woman attending me scolded, but I shook my head.

"Just a few minutes with my daughter," I assured her, annoyed.

Ilithyia crawled to the shiny copper mirror and stared sternly at her reflection until Artemis, and I moved up on either side of her and made funny faces into the metal. Then, Ilithyia giggled. Her laugh rose up in high-pitched squeals of delight that set both Artemis and me to laugh as well until a sound at the door roused us. There were harsh voices in the antechamber of my room and then booted footsteps. The girl attending me stepped back uncertainly as Hades's thin frame suddenly towered in the doorway, scowling. Artemis stiffened and reached out for Ilithyia instinctively. I scrambled to my feet.

I stood awkwardly, jewelry and gowns strewed about me and my hair half done up.

"Lucifer," I said, trying to strike a dignified pose. His intrusion into my private chamber implied an informality that should not exist. "What are you doing here?"

Hades lifted his brow and cast a scornful eye on Ilithyia and Artemis who still sat crouched by the mirror.

"It is your first high council," he said as if that was answer enough.

I struggled to regain my composure. Though I'd tried to mold myself into my new position, carrying myself with dignity and grace, I found it difficult to maintain my sense of power and control. The more I tried to tame myself the more inept I felt I became.

"I will be ready for my escort shortly," I stammered.

He lingered for a moment, his eyes running the length of my disheveled form, and then he turned abruptly and walked away without another word.

Artemis pursed her lips as I turned to her. She shook her head as she lifted Ilithyia, and pulled a warm child's cloak from the mess on the floor.

"Be wary today," she said earnestly. "And remember who you are."

I nodded, reaching out my hand to squeeze her shoulder and kiss my daughter's cheek before Artemis took her to the patio and the garden beyond. This was what my life had come to. Signaling the girl back to attend me, I slipped the jewels back on my fingers and the bracelets about my wrists, then let her bind my hair with ribbons scented in lemon and sewn with mother of pearl. I looked into the mirror when we were done and stared hard at the facade of myself. I turned to go but then hesitated, hearing Ilithyia's laughter in the garden and Artemis's warm voice encouraging. I longed to join them but turned toward the duties of my day.

Two women, I'd become accustomed to trailing me stood at attention as I entered the hall outside my rooms. They were strong women, each with a short sword and spear. I recognized them from Athena's honor guard. For a moment I pondered how Hades had been able to persuade them to let him enter. The horrible realization dawned on me then that they had respected his power and position as Lucifer more than mine.

I grew tense.

The women strode a short distance behind me as I moved down the corridor toward the gathering room where I assumed Hades waited.

When I looked into the room, I stopped. Hades was not alone. Kronos and another man sat comfortably on the plush chairs about a fire next to them. One of my attendants had brought them cheese and bread, olives and wine. They were all turned toward the flame and didn't hear me as I stepped in, and for a moment I overheard their conversation.

"She's not afraid of you," said a voice I recognized immediately as Ajax's.

I bristled. I'd come to despise the man as much as he disliked me. He stank of beer and leered at every woman.

"Afraid is a strong word," Kronos countered. "Must we speak of her so?"

"But she should be afraid, father," Hades said. "Who is she really, in the bigger scheme of things?"

I froze. Were they talking about me?

The attendant stepped back around the corner, and I took up my pace with hers, forcing a smile. The men turned smoothly and got to their feet, nodding their greeting. Kronos reached for my hand as he always did and placed it to his lips, his fine manners never forgotten. I was grateful Ajax, and Hades didn't do the same.

"You've all come to wish me well," I said dryly. "How kind."

Kronos nodded and slid my hand through his arm.

"Yes, yes my dear, and as this is your first council we wanted to escort you as befits the first lady of our house. Zeus would have come, but his duties lie with his troops today."

He moved me smoothly down the corridor to the main hall while the other two men followed behind in silence. Hades had motioned my guard away, and although they didn't desert me, as I was sure he intended, they dropped back several paces leaving me quite alone with my unwelcome escort.

Kronos chatted as we walked, asking about Ilithyia and the progress with my new additions to the temple garden. I had brought Persephone on to reclaim it, and we'd opened its doors to the women of the city. Many had taken refuge there to pray together and help rebuild the labyrinth that anchored it to the land. Still, others had mended the fountains, and I had commissioned a public bath to be built along one side.

"All goes well," I said neutrally. "We have had a bigger turnout than we expected for the full moon services, but soon the weather will be warm enough to hold them outside. What finer chapel is there than the one beneath the sky?"

I could almost feel Hades roll his eyes, while Kronos responded warmly. We continued to chat as we moved across the grand verandah and outside to our waiting horses. A full guard of temple priestesses was already mounted, and Athena held Pegasus for me at the bottom of the steps. I had not seen him since I'd left Hecate's cave and the surprise of it overcame me. I dropped Kronos's arm and almost flew down the stairs, reaching my palm to his muzzle. He gave a light whinny and hooved the ground.

"Lady," Athena said smiling, handing me the reins. "Hecate sends her blessing."

She helped me up on to Pegasus's back, my gown splaying down over his haunches like a scarlet banner. Athena got on her horse, a stunning black stallion, and called her guard around us.

Hades's horse sidled up to Pegasus.

"There's no need for all this show," Hades said, clearly annoyed.

He waved toward Ajax and the handful of Titan riders that trotted nearby. "We can vouch for the lady's safety, Athena, that is why we are here."

Athena did not move from her position at my side. Her honor guard circled their horses in formation about me. Twelve women surrounded us with their shields glistening in the sun. Their weapons lay covered by the simple black cloaks of the priestess guard.

Hades turned to me directly. "Have you no control over these women?" he said.

Pegasus whinnied, and Athena's black stallion answered, sidestepping toward Hades's horse and nudging him away.

"Don't worry," Athena snapped before I could answer, "we won't make too big a show when we arrive at the council. We'll let you make it look as though you're the ones protecting the Draconigena."

"Athena!" My voice was sharp. She snapped about to face me. I had never spoken to her in such a way before, and for a moment, I hesitated, unsure of my position, but a slight smile curled her lips.

"My apologies, Lady," she said, dipping her head low.

She signaled her women and Pegasus followed closely, forcing the Titans to fall in behind us. The politics of her actions settled on my mind as we rode. Rather than arriving surrounded by the men, I would now appear to be in the lead to those gathered outside. Her words had served to chastise them and let them know we were aware of their ploy, without the harsh sentiments coming from me directly. I'd seen her, and my grandmother plays these very same roles, Athena taking the brunt of the disgruntled party, while my grandmother appeared the peacemaker. I gripped tight to my reins and took a long breath wishing I could dig my heels into Pegasus's side and be free of this rigid role.

The council went well. I sat by Kronos, and when the time came to vote, I made sure to vote as he did. I placated his fears, not speaking too forcefully, and asked his opinion as my grandmother had counseled me to do. She sat on the opposite side of the room, and I was careful not to make eye contact with her or to vote her way. She had made certain that the matters of the day had been relatively inconsequential and she'd taken a firm stand against my own to publicly display the separation in our vote. We'd wait until the issues of evacuation and catastrophe were brought forward to use my vote in the service of our purpose. While I felt that Kronos would begin to trust me, I feared that Hades was aware of our aim; he was one Titan I didn't want to contend with.

As the full moons passed, my grandmother increased my duties, and I was forced to spend less and less time with Ilithyia and Artemis. This was not easy for me, or without consequence. As she began to crawl, I noticed Artemis's influence in the way Ilithyia mimicked the movement of animals, picking up her cloth dolls in her little mouth rather than with her hands and flapping her arms like wings when she wanted to be picked up or put down. Her first sounds resembled the rough growl of the wolf and the silly call of morning birds, but these things only made me laugh. They had grown very close, and most nights I found Artemis forgoing Aphrodite's bed to sleep with me, Ilithyia sweetly between us. It was the time I looked forward to most.

All seemed settled into a steady rhythm of formality that I thought would never be broken.

Then, one night early in spring, as the palace lay quiet, I woke from a terrible dream. My eyes flew open in the darkness, and I gasped for breath.

"Artemis!"

I pulled Ilithyia's sleeping form into my arms and quieted her as she stirred. Artemis lifted her head slowly, blinking in the dim strip of moonlight that fell in through the window.

"Artemis, get up!"

I was on my feet, reaching for a cloak when I heard hard

footsteps at the door and stirring down the hall. Artemis slid out of bed and reached for a torch by the brazier, lighting it in the flickering coals. The flame leapt as our door flew open and Athena stood before us.

"Outside!" she commanded moving toward me, and Ilithyia. She had a small guard about her. "Artemis, bring those cloaks and sandals and that flask of water."

Her hands were about my arm pulling me quickly into the hall, which was now filled with half-asleep women hurrying toward the verandah and the open garden beyond. Someone was sent to ring the warning bell at the temple, and I caught sight of my grandmother, her emerald cloak drawn close about her, and a full guard following. She stepped out beneath the moon, calling the priestesses to her.

"What is it?" Artemis was by my side. She put down my sandals so that I could step into them, and then reached for Ilithyia who looked groggily about.

"I'm not sure, but there was a sign, Artemis, I had a dream. The earth, the earth was—"

And then it came. A low, deep rumble and the ground moved beneath us. The pillars on the verandah above us shook, and the women screamed.

A jagged heat filled my heart, and my subdued facade was forgotten. I took Artemis's hand and rushed down the steps, out onto the open green, clutching Artemis and Ilithyia to me, calling the words of power and protection in a firm and commanding voice. The women around me followed. I began to chant, and they intoned with me. The earth shook again, vibrating up my legs, forcing me to step back to keep my balance, but still, my mind and heart were one, peaceful pillars of strength, and the sensation of strength seemed to move out of me to the others.

When the shaking passed, I called to the woman closest to me who had maintained her hold on a torch and bade her lift it toward the stone. A thick crack had hewn the steps, and sliced its way up the marble column. I knew this building to be one of the best built in the city, and I realized immediately that others might have fallen.

"We should gather in the labyrinth," I said to Artemis, and then turned, seeing the looks of shock and disorientation on the women's faces about me. "Go to the temple!" I cried in a commanding voice. I pointed toward my guard. "You, go ring the bell."

The woman nodded as if relieved to have direction. The others followed me to the mystic circle, the labyrinth, which lay before the temple portico. As the bell sounded, men and women came to join us from the other side of the estate. The earth trembled again, only this time much quieter, but a wave of panic moved over the group. I searched the crowd for my grandmother, but she had gone inside the temple. I turned to my guard who'd stayed close at my side, and I noticed several more of Athena's women had joined them.

"Stay with Artemis and my daughter," I commanded.

Before they could protest, I pointed at one who held a torch and signaled her to my side. I mounted the steps to the temple two at a time. The flame of the torch lit half my face as I raised my arms out to the gathering crowd to quiet their fears. I started up the earth chant, and they joined in, the familiarity of the words and the strong resonance of its sound calmed their panic.

Another short wave shook us, but this time no one moved from their space, keeping the chant strong and deep. I watched as they reached out, taking each other's hands.

Behind me, there was a sound, and my grandmother

stepped from the temple and moved to a place beside me. I could see the light of dawn beginning on the horizon behind us as she assured the crowd that the main quake was over.

Zeus and a small troop of his men rode in through the gates below us and pounded up the hill toward the circle. He was off his horse before it stopped, bounding to my side. He wrapped me in his arms.

"You're alright?"

I was aware of people watching. I pulled away and took his hands to calm him.

"All is well here, Zeus, we're safe."

He took a breath, then seemed to realize we were the people's focus. He let go of my hands and pulled himself up. He waved to his troops.

"Bring Ilithyia, and we'll take you out of the city where it's safe!" he said.

I shook my head, my power alive in me. All the women's eyes watched me. There was too much to be done now.

"Zeus, Rhea has told us the worst is over. We can trust her vision. Now, we must tend to our people. Take your troops through Caledocean and make certain the great houses open their doors to those in need. Go to the temple of healers and demand they come out into the streets to seek anyone who's been injured."

He nodded at my command and turned to Ajax, snapping the orders. Ajax hesitated, looking from his commander to me.

"Zeus, the city has its own peace-keepers," he protested. "And we can't tell the temple of healers what to do! They're priests!"

Zeus rounded on him. "My people need me!" he growled. "This is not time for politics, Ajax, you have my orders!"

Ajax stepped back, his hand on the hilt of his sword, surprise evident on his face. He moved back to his horse and shouted Zeus's instructions to the men. Zeus watched as they took their formation, then turned back to me. He stared at me for a moment, the torch in his hands casting a blood red hue across his face. I saw pride in his eyes.

"Well done, Lady," he said and dipped his head low in respect. "We shall do as you've said." He moved to his horse and mounted, pulling the stallion around hard, then kicked it forward. His men followed.

I turned to Athena then. "Send your women into the city and let it be known that anyone in need of shelter or healing may come here and we'll serve them."

She nodded but signaled for my guard. "No," I shook her off. "There is too much to do."

"No, Lady," she said leaning very close. "I will do as you command, but now, more than ever, your person must be protected." She glanced keenly toward Artemis and Ilithyia. "And they must be kept safe as well." She reached out and took hold of my arm. "Trust me, Hera."

There was no time to argue as she stepped away and her guard moved about me. Some drew close to Ilithyia and Artemis, who had gathered together a group of women with young children. Artemis was already telling them a story to keep the little ones settled.

It was a long and arduous day. I instructed my priestesses to set out soft mats in the field beneath a blue sky, for which we were all grateful. Athena's women brought dozens of wounded to them, and the healers and surgeons worked together throughout the day and long into the night.

Zeus spent the time with his men, riding patrols through Caledocean to keep the peace and spread reassurances. He thoughtfully sent a small group from his training grounds to set up tents in our field for those left without homes. As reports came to me from around the city, we were relieved that very little damage had been done. The bulk of the injured lived on the outskirts, their wood or mud-brick houses having caved in. Already, masons were being sent to make repairs, and the city council had called on the engineers to plan for rebuilding. A council had been called, but I didn't attend, helping with the healings until dusk, tending to so many who'd been hurt. Demeter opened our stores of grain and saw to feeding the gathering, while Persephone and Artemis erected a tent for the children. I could make out where they were throughout the day by the black-cloaked women that surrounded them.

At sunset, my grandmother returned from the great council with a large number of lords and ladies in her company. She stood before the temple and gathered us about her.

"The earth has settled," she announced. "It is safe to return to your homes."

I realized then that the earth hadn't shaken for more than half the day.

"The council will make all efforts to rebuild those houses and shops that have been damaged, but it will take some time. Until then, those without a home may stay here with the priestesses. And let us make no mistake that this is a sign. The decade of change is before us," she cried out to the crowd. "The prophecy will come to pass. This is only the warning."

She turned to the priests that had gathered from the various temples, and to their lords and ladies, and spoke in a cold, even tone. "The earth is shifting in the sea. There are so many of us now that it will take years to bring all to safety. We need more ships built to take our people to safer shores.

New cities and towns must be founded and soon. For the time has come—Atlantis must be abandoned."

There was a great commotion, and the nobles standing next to her shook their heads and frowned. Hades stepped forward and took a place on the steps opposite Rhea. He was very well dressed and groomed, and his left hand sparkled with jewels. I shook my head at the thought of what he must have been doing all day while so many were in need. The nobles around him seemed not to notice, or care. Most seemed relieved to see him.

"Friends!" Hades cried out in a conciliatory manner. "These are matters for the high council to decide on! And the council has been wise in its decision of our course. Expand first, so that we have a place to evacuate to, should the need arise."

"The need has already arisen!" A man's voice rose up out of the crowd. "Last night was a warning as the priestesses say. The prophecy—"

"The earth shakes everywhere!" Hades cried out. "There is no place where the people are free from tremors. Should we let this one incidence frighten us into leaving? Are you ready to abandon your homes, and your livelihoods? Where will we go? To the tribes?" He lifted his brows and laughed outright. "The tribes know nothing of our way of life. The only heights their civilizations have attained are the ones we've given them! Since we've opened a trade route from Anatolia to the southern tip of the great continent, they've begun to form sprawling, lawless communities. Three and four thousand people in fortified villages, living no better than the animals they raise!"

"Better to live simply, with animals, and be alive!" another man called out.

There was a surge of assent, but Hades didn't back down. His lips curled into a thin smile. He stepped toward the crowd and nodded, reaching out his hands in a quieting gesture as one would with a group of frightened children.

"The council will keep us all alive," he said emphatically. "The council has taken every measure to secure land for our people, outside of Atlantis, as is prudent. We are building our own city there, bringing our advanced way of life with us. If there are more signs in the future, we'll have a place to go, a new Atlantis. But should we run now? Should we give in to fear?" He shook his head. "As the Lucifer, light bearer of the Titan Temple of Light, I say no! We shall be humble before the earth, and make peace with her and rebuild our homes! And the earth will bless us for many more generations."

People shifted on their feet and many murmured assent. The nobles were visibly turning away from my grandmother's side in Hades's direction with relief evident on their faces.

"But the priestesses were outside before anyone even knew the quake was coming!" a woman shouted. "They have their ways of knowing, and it would be prudent for us to follow such wisdom as they offer."

There were general murmurs and nods of agreement.

"Yes," Hades cried out, "it's true; the priestesses were gathered outside, safely, while the rest of us were still vulnerable in our beds! They may have the gift of knowing, but it was used to their benefit, not ours!"

There were cries of protest and anger, and someone yelled out that there wasn't enough time, that they were going to ring the bell, but I could feel the tension rising in the air. Hades's smile broadened. He held up his arms one more time.

"The question I leave you with is this: If the priestesses really *could* save us, then why didn't they?"

He had planted his seed of doubt in the fertile soil of fearful minds. I looked up at Rhea and saw that she knew it too.

"The priestesses have always served the interests of our people," she said, but her voice was tired, and I could hear the resignation in her tone. "We have given our warning and a clear plan for evacuation. But the choice will always be in the hands of the council..."

We were all too tired to confront this. I rolled down my sleeves and pulled my cloak about me. Priestesses lit the rushlights and handed out candles through the crowd. I made my way to my grandmother's side to see if I could help, but she shook her head and turned away from the crowd. The skin beneath her eyes was dark and swollen, and she rubbed her temples as she walked away. When we were alone beneath the temple arches, she turned to me, her face grave.

"I've heard the earth speak and seen the visions in the scrying bowl," she said. "But I cannot make another share my experience, or act upon that certainty." She laid a hand on mine. "There was a time, Hera when a priest's and priestess' word was trusted. Now, as one of us falls from the light, so do we all." She said this last with her eyes intent on Hades who continued talking in warm, charming tones to his gathered group of elites.

The night wore on. A messenger came from Zeus to tell me he was needed at camp with his men, and so I turned from the temple and walked up the hill to my rooms. When I got there, Artemis was not in bed, but sleeping on a mat outside in the garden covered in thick furs, my daughter tucked gently beneath her arm. A woman I recognized stood guard just beyond the wall of roses, a thick spear held at the ready. Another was outside my door.

I turned back into the room to bathe and dress more warmly before I joined them beneath the stars, but to my surprise, my grandmother and Athena stood in the door. Rhea walked up to me and glanced over my shoulder at the two forms in the blankets outside. Her face was drawn and pale, but she forced a smile.

"That one takes no chances," she said, nodding toward Artemis. "That is good."

I nodded, moving wearily to the bench and table that someone had laid out with figs and cheese. I poured a goblet of wine with no water. I'd not had time to eat all day. Rhea and Athena joined me, and I poured wine for them as well. We sipped and ate in silence. A girl came to tend the hearth, and I bade her build it high so that it cast fine light upon us as we dined. She also lit candles and poured warm water into a bowl where we washed our hands when we were done.

"You did well, today, Hera," Rhea said then. "You've integrated the teachings well, representing peace in the face of great danger. I'm proud of you."

I smiled through my exhaustion. I was surprised at how her words pleased me. She spoke of other things then, of how the tremors would continue and then wane and her fear that the people would not take the threat seriously enough. Hades and the Titan line would lead the council toward vigorous expansion efforts, which meant war.

"But why?" I asked wearily. "Why don't we just begin to take our people to safety now?"

"The longer we wait, the more time the dynasty kings and priests have to set up powerful empires of their own outside of Atlantis. Doing it this way assures them wealth, power and control, Hera."

I leaned back and slid my hands behind my neck, shutting my eyes. My body ached, and even the wine hadn't warmed me. The responsibility of bringing our people to safety weighed heavier on me now that I'd felt and seen only this small display of the earth's power. And now Hades had made clear he would oppose me at every turn.

Athena shifted loudly in her seat opposite me, and I opened my eyes. She was staring at me intently.

"We must speak of something else," she said.

I remembered her words earlier and the closeness of my guard, but it was my grandmother who spoke.

"Everyone knows you are the Draconigena, Hera. Now with this quake…word will travel fast and those that believe the prophecy will know that the signs are complete and the end times are near."

She looked out at the garden for a moment, a light breeze moving over us. I followed her gaze, and my eyes rested on the peaceful scene of Artemis and Ilithyia.

"The holy oil cannot be destroyed, Hera, and for those who know it exists, it will stand to reason that you are its guardian. It is the Dragon of Atlantis, and there are many who would take it for their own."

Athena pulled her stool closer to me, scraping it across the stones. She leaned in as if someone could hear us.

"They will seek out ways to gain power over you, Hera. Since you're so strong in your intuition and have the skill of the fire, they'll pose no direct threat *to* you. It is through the people you love that they will seek power *over* you."

"What?" I exclaimed. "What are you saying? Is Ilithyia in danger?"

Rhea shook her head. "Athena has a devoted group pledged to your safety. You must trust her and allow her to guard and protect the ones you love."

"We've even sent women to your village," Athena added. "They will look out for any signs of trouble and alert your father and mother."

My eyes grew wide, and I threw my hand over my open mouth. The ones I loved in danger? Tears fell down my cheeks, and I shook my head.

"You should've told me this before—" but I stopped there, knowing my words were useless. This was my destiny, and these were its terms.

They sat patiently by my side as I wiped at my cheeks with the back of my hand. I filled another goblet of wine. Then my grandmother continued. She offered me a plan of protection that tightened about my heart, but I nodded as she spoke, for it was a wise course of action. I should send Ilithyia to be raised at the Emerald Temple. She would be safe there and could grow up free of fear. I could split my time between the Emerald Temple, and here at the Titan palace. I could claim the temple here on the grounds as my own. It could become again, the Temple of the Rose, an extension of the Emerald Temple, here on the Titan estate.

"The Temple of the Rose was once used for such a purpose, and now we can bring it to life once again. It's the perfect opportunity to bring our women here. We will have the presence of priestesses here, in the city."

I nodded. I'd already seen the powerful effect our presence here had on the women of Caledocean. More were coming to pray at the Temple of the Rose every day.

"You would spend part of your time with Ilithyia at the Emerald Temple, and the rest here with doing temple business. And of course, there is Zeus," Rhea said. "He has a strong loyalty to you, Hera. That is a good thing."

"Yes, I suppose it is," I said.

I rose to my feet and paced to the window my back to them both.

Athena spoke again, but her tone softened. "And you must have another child," she said, "A boy, a Titan heir, whom you'll leave here in their charge. They will give him power as he grows, and protect him. Zeus *must* have a son."

I frowned. Two children, neither to be reared by own hands and heart? For the first time, I glimpsed an understanding of my parents' protection of me. How could my life have come to this? Even before they were finished speaking, I knew it was the course I would take.

I turned back to them, lifted my head and set my jaw firmly.

"I will do it, to protect Ilithyia," I said, nodding my agreement.

When they left me, I moved back to my seat as the fire dwindled in the hearth. My eyes rested outside upon the nest of furs beneath the stars and, upon it, the two souls I loved most in the world.

CHAPTER ELEVEN

IN THE AFTERMATH OF THE QUAKE, Zeus required more of my time. He wanted me with him as he traveled through the city, meeting men and women from the crafts guilds and merchant quarter. His charismatic personality made him a friend to all. We spent the week meeting with healers and surgeons, architects and builders, horse breeders and bull riders.

"Zeus, by the next full moon, we'll know everyone in the city by name," I teased.

He smiled at that and noted it as a good idea. "People follow the ones they know and love," he said. "What my brother on the hill does not seem to understand is that true power comes from being well-liked."

I stiffened at the talk of power; the only subject men wished to speak of these days. Zeus helped me into his chariot and drove us down the long cobbled street to the port where we climbed out and mounted the small hill that overlooked the sea. His vast training grounds were spread below us on the beach and bluffs beyond. A small town of its own seemed to be growing up around it.

Men came from all parts of Atlantis to take up service with Zeus. His troops were swelling in number. He never tired of talking about this, and how he had begun to erect a military training ground in the long sand dunes by the harbor. He showed me his handiwork with pride, pointing out each station—the archers, spear guards, cavalry, and swordsmen. Zeus made certain his troops took part in every aspect of his army's growth and provision.

"How will you feed such a force?" I asked.

He pointed to the long row of fishing boats strung along the shore.

"We'll need this force for the expansion," he declared as we sat aloft the hill gazing down on the busy scene below. "The other dynasties will rally about us when they see my army at work."

"And when will that be?" I asked as I slid my arm through his and lay my head on his shoulder.

He wrapped his arm around me.

"When the ranks are full, and the ships are built," he said evenly, his eyes on the horizon. "It will be several years yet, but it takes that much time to train an army. Then we shall need a quest, a proving ground for our strength. When that is accomplished, Hera, you will have no problem rallying the support you need for your evacuation efforts. They will fall in line when they see what we can do."

A dark sense of foreboding passed over me as he spoke. A proving ground for his *troops? The others falling in line?* I was not naive enough to think that wars would never be fought, but were there people who would fight just for the fight itself? I thought of Ajax then, and Hades, and I shivered. Zeus pulled me beneath his cloak and turned to look at me.

"What's wrong?"

I shook my head. How could I explain? He slid his hand down to my hips and pulled me closer, leaning down to kiss me. His lips were warm and gentle, and his eyes were filled with wanting as he pulled away to look at me.

"It's time I came back to your bed," he said.

I thought of Ilithyia and Artemis, and the closeness we shared. There were many nights Artemis sung us both to sleep.

Zeus slid both hands down to my hips, sending desire through my limbs.

"Your body's more beautiful than ever, Hera," he said, kissing me deeply this time. "You're healed, my love. You're strong now and settled into our new life. It's time."

I tilted my head and looked long into his eyes searching. "Soon," I said.

I leaned in to entice another kiss, but he held me back. His eyes brooded.

"Artemis cares so well for Ilithyia, she won't mind if you slip away tonight—"

His hands found my breasts, and I caught my breath. "You've stopped nursing," he said.

"Yes, but—"

"I want you, Hera. I need you. Our union may have been political, but I swear to you, my need is real."

I sighed as his lips found my neck, and the warm urge to have him rose up into my legs. My mouth quivered. My arms slid behind his neck, and I wrapped my hands into his thick hair. My body stirred, and he responded.

"Soon," I said. "I have to get Ilithyia and Artemis settled," I answered.

He bit my shoulder playfully and laughed out loud. I could see he was satisfied with my answer, and we turned again toward the sea and watched the sun paint its way across the sky.

When we returned to the palace, I kissed Zeus goodbye. The guards stepped aside as I passed into my rooms, scattered with toys, and came upon Artemis playing happily with my daughter in the garden outside. They were both wearing the same thin, black robes, Ilithyia standing at the edge of a stone bench holding onto its sides. I stopped in the doorway and smiled, watching as she reached her small hand out to Artemis, grasping at the air. Artemis held out her arms only a few feet away encouraging the child to step forward into her waiting hands. Ilithyia was tentative. She bobbed up and down and grasped impatiently at the space between them. Suddenly I heard her little voice, high and clear. "Mama," she said.

My smile faded.

"Mama, Mama," she said again, pleased with herself.

Artemis laughed but shook her head. "No," she answered scooping Ilithyia up in her arms. "I'm not Mama."

She must have heard me move in the doorway for she looked up, startled, and pointed at me. "There's your Mama," she said, moving toward me.

Ilithyia giggled, her round face alive with mischief. She held her arms out to me. I lifted her up, squeezing her too tightly to my chest. She rebelled by trying to wriggle away. Feelings of loss and disappointment welled in my chest, but I couldn't find any words.

"She'll say it again," Artemis said hesitantly.

I could sense her discomfort. I tried to smile, but I could feel tears welling in my eyes. The guilt from my decision to send Ilithyia away bore down on me.

I hugged my child. Ilithyia still struggled in my grasp and flapped her arms to get down, but I clung to her all the more.

In another moment she squawked and growled. I resignedly set her down on the grass. She latched onto my leg, pulling herself upright and took a wobbly step in Artemis's direction. She flapped her arms again, looking up into my friend's face, which had lost its usual serenity.

Artemis shook her head. "I have to go now," she told Ilithyia, lifting her and placing her back in my arms. "You stay here with Mama."

An odd moment passed between us as I took back my child and watched Artemis turn and walk away. Ilithyia pointed at Artemis as she went, struggling in my arms and crying out in an agitated tone, as though she wished to run after her. My heart clenched, and I had the urge to let her go after Artemis. Yet as I turned and stepped into the garden with her, cooing and humming her name, she quieted and gripped onto my tunic. When I put her down she fixed her eyes on the flowers with excitement, all irritation forgotten.

We played together beneath the trees, the sunlight dappling her cheeks as she rolled in the leaves and giggled. I fed her mashed fruit from her wooden bowl, and she gulped warm milk from a real cup. When the wind picked up, chilling our faces with its bluster, I reached out to her. She stood alone for a moment as if leaning against the wind. Then she lifted her arms to me. "Mama," she said.

I leaned down pulling her into my arms.

"Yes," I whispered. "Yes, my beautiful girl."

That night, I lay with Ilithyia alone in the dark listening to her steady breathing and stroking her thick head of curls. It was not yet late, and the candles still glowed bright, but it was long past the time Artemis was usually curled up beside us. I was relieved when she finally stepped into the room. She stood by the door for a long time as if she were unsure of whether she should come in. I lay very still watching her silhouette until she turned quietly as if to leave.

"Don't go," I said.

She stood near the doorway without moving. "I shouldn't," she answered. "She's old enough now, and you should bring Zeus to your bed. She hardly knows him." Her tone was sad.

I slid lightly off the bed and went to Artemis. I took her hand and led her across the room to the couch by the window where the soft moonlight illuminated her face. I could see thin lines of concern between her brows. It took me a few moments to find the right words and my throat was tight as I spoke, but I told her all that my grandmother and Athena had advised.

"Rhea wants to take her soon," I said. "But I don't want Rhea to raise her, Artemis. You should be the one."

She sat very still, but the look on her face changed. Her eyes glistened, but she shook her head.

"It's a wise plan, Hera, and necessary for Ilithyia's safety, but I'm not a priestess, and your grandmother will insist on such a thing if I were to remain at the Emerald Temple."

Good, I thought, she hadn't said she wouldn't do it! She must know as I did that her destiny was with my child. We were bound together.

I took up her hands in mine and spoke intently. "This isn't my grandmother's decision," I said resolutely. "I want you to be Ilithyia's guardian, Artemis. You're my dearest and most trusted friend, and I love you."

She softened at this. "A place will be made for you at the temple, and I'll make certain Ili answers only to you when I'm not there."

I paused and let this sink in. The wind blew gently through the tree outside the uncovered window, and we both turned, letting the warm breeze brush our faces. She smiled, and I continued.

"And it's not like you'd suffer for companionship," I said slyly. "It is an island of women, after all—"

She blushed at that and pushed my hands away lightly. Then she stood and paced the room. I knew her well enough to understand that she needed a long silence that followed. I stared up at the starry night sky and waited.

She moved to the bed and looked down on Ilithyia, and I moved to her side. She reached for my hand. "I will keep her safe," she said.

I took a deep breath and smiled.

Yes, I thought. *And you'll keep her wild and make her fierce, so they'll never be able to tame her. Make my child your own, Artemis, and between us, we shall raise a priestess who will know how to be free.*

CHAPTER TWELVE

LONG AFTER ARTEMIS HAD CRAWLED into bed beside Ilithyia and fallen asleep, I lay wakeful and restless in the moonlight. All my education in the mystic arts hadn't prepared me to accept this invisible constriction of my life. I had lost my sense of self and felt adrift in an ocean of duty. I was a woman now, but so often I still felt as powerless as a child. I could see that my grandmother was pleased with all we had accomplished, but she and the others didn't respect me, not really. They were controlling me. As I lay there, I realized I wasn't sure if I'd *given* my voice to them or if they had *taken* it on purpose. Either way, I knew that the more I had acquiesced some essential quality had been buried inside of me, and I wanted it back.

I slipped quietly from beneath the blankets, and pulled on my scarlet cape, then crept out of the room. There were two women posted outside the door as usual. They were surprised to see me, but in a moment, Laura, the leader, was at my side with her spear at the ready. I waved her away.

"I'm only going to Zeus's apartments," I assured her.

"I'll go with you, Lady, and Ellen will stay here to watch

over your daughter," she said. "Athena's orders. It's for your own protection."

I nodded resentfully. "Of course," I said.

Was there nothing I could do in privacy?

The halls were dimly lit, and attendants still milled about with casks of wine and firewood. As I passed the Megaron, the room we feasted in, people were still scattered about lifting trays and moving chairs. I pulled my cloak closer about me, but each person I passed recognized me, nodding in deference. A few cast knowing smiles at me as I crossed from my wing of the palace into the men's quarters where Zeus had elaborate rooms of his own. There were other well-appointed quarters for guests; Hades and Kronos kept suites here as well.

I hesitated a moment in the dim passage looking for Zeus's door. A latch sounded nearby, and I recognized one of Zeus's attendants stepping into the hall with a heavy bucket of wood. He took several steps down the hall toward a large door, then saw me and stopped abruptly.

"Lady," he murmured awkwardly, "Lady, what are you—" but then he seemed to remember himself. He dipped his head.

I nodded, looking up above the door. The light of my guard's torch sent a striking flash across Zeus's lightning bolt carved into the heavy stone. Before I could fully take in the moment, or ponder why an attendant would be bringing fresh wood to the master at this hour of the night, I reached for the handle and pushed hard.

The room was large and lavish. Drapes, drawn closed, hung from the side of the bed. Candles burned low all about the room. The signs of feasting lay about: several empty goblets, broken bread and a plate of half eaten fruit. I saw Zeus's gold skirt strewn across the floor and his doeskin boots beside the brazier. An odd chill ran over me. My guard had stopped by the door, but I could feel her peering in behind me, and Zeus's own attendant stood frozen in the doorway.

I reached for a torch on the wall without thinking. When I glanced back to the room, my eyes came to rest on the piece of fabric draped over the couch in the corner, its folds of silk glistening in the candlelight. I walked over to it, fingering the fine red pattern embroidered into its folds.

It was a woman's dress. On the table beside it lay two pearl earrings and a necklace fashioned from copper.

With a shaking hand, I turned to the bed and pulled back the drape.

The light from my torch spilled down like a wave of orange, illuminating the woman's long tresses that fell loose over Zeus's naked body.

"How dare you," I said under my breath.

With the torch in one hand, I reached down with the other, grabbing a handful of the woman's hair, pulling hard. She came awake with a shriek as I dragged her from the bed waving the flames above her with a deadly feeling. From the corner of my eye I saw Zeus leap from the bed, grasping for his blade, but when he saw me and registered what was happening, he rushed for the torch that shook in my hand. When I felt his grip tight on my wrist, I pressed against him with an uncommon strength that sent him stumbling past the posts of the bed.

"How dare you shame me like this!" I cried. "In my own house and after insisting I bring you to my bed!"

The woman tried to crawl past me toward her dress, but I reached down and took her by the hair again, raising her to her feet. She whimpered as I pressed her toward the door.

I heard Zeus's voice calling my name, and felt him reach for me again, but I swung the torch toward him with a furious intent that sent him scrambling across the room. The woman shrieked, but I tightened my grip, pulling her face close to my own. I recognized her as the young wife of a man who sat on the council. I tossed her, naked, into the hallway. My guard stepped back, her eyes wide, hand on her blade. I sent her a deadly look, and she stayed where she was. Zeus's attendant had dropped the bucket, logs spilling across the threshold. I could feel the heat rising from my limbs. My mouth curved to say the words, to call on the fire, and my limbs ached for the release.

The woman stood in the hallway, shaking, trying to cover her nakedness, her eyes wild.

"Go!" I hissed.

She cried out and covered her breasts as she backed away from me. At last, she scampered down the hall. There was noise down the corridor, and people emerged from their rooms, but I hardly noticed. Turning back into the room I saw Zeus by the brazier, naked and confused. I could see the dim look of consternation on his face, and then apprehension took hold. Heat moved all the way across the room from my body toward him. He held up his hand as if to protect himself. "Hera, put out the torch, please," he said.

I moved slowly toward him; my jaw clenched too tight to speak.

He stepped backward, away from me. "Hera you said I'd have to wait, that soon you'd call for me. It was out of respect that I—"

"Respect!" I took another step forward as he retreated again. He grasped at his skirt as he went, wrapping it hastily about his waist.

There was a rush of movement behind me and as I spun around, Hades, half dressed, his hair disheveled, stood in the doorway with Aphrodite beside him. He held the stricken woman I'd thrown from the room tight by the wrist as she writhed in his grasp, her naked form cringing. Aphrodite, her hair unbound and loose about the light robe that clung tight to her, slid her arm through his. Her eyes roamed lightly over the scene.

Zeus's attendant was gone and my guard out of sight.

"What is this?" Hades demanded, but as he took in the scene, it became evident that no one needed to answer.

The woman continued to try and wrench herself from Hades's grasp, but he held her firmly as if she were a plaything he dangled before me. His cold eyes met mine, and I shook with anger.

"Get out!" I raged. "Get out, get out!"

Without thought of the others, of the poor woman in his arms, or Aphrodite who I'd already hurt with such irresponsible reaction, I sent a wave of heat from the torch toward Hades. His hair moved back from his face, and the woman shrieked again. Aphrodite let go of his arms and leapt outside the room, but Hades only narrowed his eyes.

"Ah, the Draconigena has power," he said smoothly. "And will you use it to scar my face too?"

He let go of the woman, who ran from the room wailing.

Zeus called out my name again, and this time I heard the desperation in his voice, but I was too far-gone in my rage. Tears spilled down my cheeks, not of sadness or grief, but the release of long-held back frustration.

My hand shook and sent the torchlight running across the wall and Hades's face. He spoke to me again in a degrading tone, but I didn't hear the words. Sweat broke hot across my brow. The light shone in his eyes, piercing the black center and I felt myself falling into them in a strange shimmering wave of heat.

I saw beyond him then. Hades's pain rose up in my mind, and I perceived the reason for his harsh tone and hatred. *I am afraid of death.* I heard the words as though he'd spoken them.

"Your fear will be the undoing of us all, Hades." I heard the words loud and clear before I realized that I had spoken them. His look became uneasy. I moved toward him again, but this time he stepped back, out into the hall, his eyes for the first time unsure. His mouth was slightly open, and I saw his bottom lip tremble before he clenched his jaw.

I caught sight of Athena and her women pushing through a throng of faces now gathered about us, but they seemed somehow far away.

"Beware, Lucifer, I will not endure your disrespect," I said in the same tone.

He looked around uncertainly, and I saw him shiver, but in a moment, he straightened and lifted his head.

"You dare to threaten me?" he cried, his arms lifting like the wings of a bat. "Have you the courage, then, to face the true might of the temple of light? We have one hundred priests, Hera, one hundred—"

A chilling sound escaped my lips as I moved toward him, the torch a blur of orange at my side.

"Do not think to hide behind your priests, Hades! It is not I that lacks courage. I know the truth. I am immortal. I am free." My voice welled up and echoed through the corridor, the crowd stepping back. "You are imprisoned by the mistaken belief that you can ever die! You are the one that is afraid, Hades, and I will no longer allow you to impress yourself upon me, this house, or my people."

"You are a fool, then," he spat. "If you stand against me, you will stand alone!"

I felt the heat cooling on my hands and cheeks. I turned to Zeus, who stood close at my side, his face pale.

"Remove your brother from my house," I said evenly.

He opened his mouth as if to speak, then closed it as he pulled himself up and nodded. He moved toward Hades and took firm hold of his arm. Kronos, who had just appeared beside Hades, began to protest.

"And your father as well!" I commanded.

Kronos looked as if I'd struck him. He turned toward Athena who had pressed her way to my side. She stared back at him intently.

"The Draconigena has spoken," she said.

Kronos blustered angry words, and I heard Hades's voice as Zeus and his man led them back down the corridor, "Take your hands off me," Hades cried. "How can you choose *her* over *me*? This is a mistake you'll always regret, Zeus, always!" Then their sound was muffled as they disappeared into their rooms.

Athena's women dispersed the crowd, but I knew the story would be spread throughout Caledocean by morning. I didn't care.

Athena took firm hold of my arm, and I let her guide me back into Zeus's room. She glanced about taking in the obvious scene. Then she moved quickly, opening the windows, allowing a fresh breeze move in around me. Dousing the candles, she reached for the torch, but I waved her away. I crossed to the hearth and tossed the torch in myself. She drew a pitcher of water to the table.

"Place your hands in it."

"Thank you, Athena," I said. "But I'll tend to myself."

Her head snapped in my direction, and I smiled.

"You've taught me well," I said, "but my time has come."

She moved to the seat beside me, shaking her head. "It is my duty—"

"No. I won't be a prisoner, afraid to be myself in the face of the life I've chosen," I said. "You've made me High Priestess and queen. There's no going back."

There was a grave silence between us, but she bowed her head and rose to her feet.

"You will take Ilithyia and Artemis to the Emerald Temple at daybreak," I instructed. "I've named Artemis, my daughter's guardian. You will make her welcome, and see to her needs."

Athena looked at me thoughtfully, but she did not object. "Is there anything else?"

I stared up into her eyes and held her gaze. Her look softened.

"That will be all," I said evenly.

"And so it shall be done," she replied.

Athena stepped forward and kneeled before me for the first time, lifting the hem of my robe to her lips. I sat quietly and let her make the respectful gesture. Then she stood and left the room.

When Zeus returned, he was composed. I watched him as he moved about the room, collecting his clothes, and his sword, placing them in a pile on a chair by the hearth. He shivered and reached for a long woolen shirt. Stretching out his big arms, he pulled the thick shirt over his head. His hair fell in soft curls about his weary face. When he was done, he sat down in the chair beside me, his hands resting lightly on the armrests. Leaning back, he exhaled loudly. He eyed me for a moment before he spoke.

"You are a fury," he said, shaking his head. "And I am ashamed that I've called you to it."

I said nothing, but something in his tone told me he was lying. He was not ashamed at all. His eyes were filled with something else, something like delight and pride. He liked how heated I'd become! Zeus was happy that I'd made this scene so that everyone would imagine me a jealous wife. But was I jealous? Was that the source of my rage?

I was growing tired now, and the anger had subsided. I thought back over the day and my earlier words to Zeus telling him I would share my bed again, soon... What had I expected all these months? I had assumed he'd taken lovers when he was far afield, and that hadn't bothered me, but to find the woman in his bed—such disrespect! That was what had enraged me so. How could he have been so thoughtless and careless in my own house?

"Hera," Zeus said then, his tone sounding well practiced. "Hera, you know I treasure you. You are the only woman I've ever loved."

I studied him for a moment, the thin lines of pride creasing around his eyes. Yes, he treasured me, the way he cherished his horse and his title as king.

It was a hard thing to let myself see.

"You know what I'm saying is true," he continued, "I love you, I do." He leaned forward in the chair earnestly, but his voice was still soft. "You will always be first in my heart, I can swear that, but I cannot be faithful."

The words were the most honest he'd ever spoken to me. I smiled at him, despite myself.

"Never in my house," I said slowly, "or when you are in

my company. Never with my women or those who live close to me."

He lifted his hand to his mouth and ran it over the stubble of his chin, and nodded. "Done."

The fire settled into a glow of embers, and I yawned, my body finally cooling in the night. I glanced at the bed and the green dress still splayed across the chair beside it. My stomach tightened. I looked around the room and its apparent signs of romance and confronted the reality of my situation. Zeus would never be the kind of man I could trust or have pride in. He was reckless and thoughtless and had married me because of what I represented to him—a fine prize, an elevated status—rather than out of true love. Oh, I was sure he *believed* he loved me, but I doubted Zeus would ever know what real love was; he would never be able to see beyond his own needs long enough to put someone else's heart first.

And then the real shock hit me. I didn't really care. I wasn't in love with Zeus, either. He wasn't a man with a noble heart and in the end that was the only thing that mattered to me.

As lonely as this realization was, it also freed me.

"I will need time," I said.

He nodded.

"And then I will give you a son, Zeus. And he will be raised by you and will be your heir."

His face creased with pleasure. He clearly had not expected this after such a scene, but I didn't stop there. I rose slowly to my feet and looked down at him.

"And then I will be free of our pledge and the question of who shares *my* bed. Understand me, Zeus, I will be faithful to you until our son is born, after which, my bed shall be my own."

The pleasure drained from his face. Yet what could he do but nod his agreement?

I moved toward the door, and he got to his feet and followed. He reached out for my hand before I opened it, and stepped closer to me, putting my palm on his chest just over his heart. I could feel it beating beneath my hand.

"I'm sorry," he said.

"I know."

"In the future—"

"Don't speak of the future, Zeus. I will not change my mind."

I looked up into his eyes, which were pale blue and unhappy. For a moment I saw the old image from my dream, the same eyes only darker blue and they pierced the wall that was being constructed about my heart. I shook the image away and stared back at Zeus sadly. He was not the man from my dreams.

I pulled my hand away from his heart and walked away.

The Story Continues in
PRIESTESS RISING
Book Three of The Priestess Chronicles
Available Now At:
www.JulienDuBrow.com

For more information about the author and Sacred Healing or to receive updates on Julien's new books and offerings sign up for her newsletter at: www.JulienDuBrow.com

AUTHOR'S NOTES

In writing this book, I have explored a myth-making process in which I imagined a time before the concept of God existed. I've always wondered what compelled our species to create the concept of an all-powerful being or beings, and I've often pondered how this being became gendered. As a scholar of mythology and mysticism, I've found that the oldest texts, songs, hymns and sacred poetry from around the world refer to an experience of unity as the primary and enduring reality. Even the mystics symbolize their experiences through gender and analogy. Thus, in writing my own myth, I've presented the central divine experience as unity and used the Minoan and Mycenaean cultures that lived 2600-1100 B.C. to create an entirely fictional time-period, in a setting that lives somewhere between myth and reality.

While it is a work of fantasy I've used the storylines of western culture's Greek Pantheon to craft this tale and in so doing, I feel it is important to share a brief description of their creation story and the true origins of their Goddess, Hera. The primary sources of the information below are Edith Hamilton's book, *Mythology*, and Vicki Noble's groundbreaking book, *The Double Goddess*.

Greek Mythology:

Ancient Greek civilization is generally acknowledged as the foundation of western culture. The Greeks reached a high level of sophistication in their philosophy, art, science and political life. The aspect of their civilization that intrigues me the most is their mythology, which pervaded their daily lives. Many of their myths date back to the pre-Greek cultures. These people lived in a matriarchal society and worshiped the Great Goddess, or Earth Mother, who represented fertility and the cycle of the seasons and the wondrous mysteries of life and death. This goddess had a consort who was linked with the starry heavens and who became the Sky God, Zeus. The Great Goddess was then Hellenized by the Greeks into the goddess Gaia, and her daughter Rhea.

The Greek Creation Myth:

In early Greece, the mythology was handed down by a strong oral tradition, until the time of Hesiod's *Theogony* in the eighth century BCE. Hesiod's telling of the Greek creation myth begins with Gaia, the Great Goddess of the earth emanating from Chaos, and thus the world begins. Chaos also births Uranus, the embodiment of the sky. Gaia and Uranus then mate. They have many offspring, two of which are Rhea and Kronos. Uranus devours his offspring until his son, Kronos, outwits him. Kronos mates with Rhea, and also devours his offspring until his son, Zeus, outwits him. Zeus then marries his sister, Hera, and divides the universe into three parts, giving his elder brother, Poseidon the sea, his brother Hades the underworld while he becomes the ruler of heaven and earth.

Hera:

Hera has been portrayed in western culture as Zeus's wife and sister. She was raised by the Titans Oceanus and Tethys, and Ilithyia (or Eileithyia) was her daughter. In Greek mythology, she is presented as the protector of marriage and married women, and most accounts describe her as a jealous wife with a wicked temper and very little compassion.

This is the image that the western world has perpetuated of the queen of the gods, and yet, in my research, I've found that this couldn't be further from the truth. Recent archeological finds now make it clear that Hera *predates* Zeus. She was venerated long before the sky god appeared. It is now thought that the worshipers of Zeus conquered the early Greek tribes that worshiped the goddess, and had their sky god (Zeus) marry the mother goddess (Hera) in order to bring him into the people's new worship. Over time, Greek authors change Hera's role of beloved mother protector to that of a jealous wife.

Before Zeus, Hera was known as the double goddess, the mother, nurturer, and wisdom keeper. Somos was the Greek isle dedicated to her teachings, and her temple still stands there today.

Although the Greeks consistently tell stories of Hera's angry nature, they couldn't hide how deeply venerated she was. We see this primarily in the fact that there are more temples built in her honor throughout Greece than any other god or goddess.

When reading the mythological tales of Hera, and comparing them with the evidence of her superior worship and ancient status, I couldn't help but notice that the Greek men writing their culture's histories had changed and maligned the character and stature of this mother goddess. This led me, and my storyline, to the usurper god, Zeus, and his motives for changing Hera's true story. Their relationship mirrors the fall of matriarchic living and the rise of patriarchy in the western world. Also, it gave me a backdrop to explore the remarkable invention of the God and the Goddess.

ACKNOWLEDGMENTS

I give thanks to my remarkable family and friends. You have held me through my own journey of healing and awakening. You have been a light in my life, and I am deeply grateful.

To Martin, who has stood by side in the light and dark moments of my life, holding up the torch of love that has so often been my guide... thank you, dearest. With all my heart, thank you.

To my teachers, I bow in gratitude for the gifts you have so generously given. I carry your teachings, your strength, and compassion within me, forever. Thank you.

And to all who will read these chronicles—I thank you for your support and wish you love and kinship on your journey.

My heart is with you.

Julien